CW00551658

Praise for Adria...

'The novel succeeds on its own [...] terms, conjuring a deep and strange sense of stillness that hints at a discomfiting truth: this is a material world and we are merely passing through it' *Sunday Times*

'The Irish Sebald' *Bookseller*

'Many have seen the tendency among Irish writers, from Joyce and Beckett up to Eimear McBride, towards experimentation as originating in this sense of foundational linguistic dispossession. Duncan proves himself to be one of the most subtle explorers of this condition writing today' *Literary Review*

'A masterful meditation on exile … by one of our most original writers' *Irish Independent*

'His sentences are unfussy, but they suddenly open out into descriptively magnificent things … It's the kind of work that makes you remember why you read' *Sunday Business Post*

'At the very forefront of writing in Ireland' *Irish Times*

'Adrian Duncan writes with emotional accuracy and what seems like effortless precision about work and exile, about buildings and cities. To his narratives, he brings a mixture of the exact and the visionary. To his characters, he brings a rawness of feeling combined with an urgent need for them to make sense of the world' Colm Tóibín

ALSO BY ADRIAN DUNCAN

Little Republics: The Story of Bungalow Bliss (non-fiction)

The Geometer Lobachevsky

Midfield Dynamo (short stories)

A Sabbatical in Leipzig

Love Notes from a German Building Site

THE GORGEOUS INERTIA OF THE EARTH

ADRIAN DUNCAN

TUSKAR ROCK PRESS

First published in Great Britain in 2025 by
Tuskar Rock Press,
an imprint of Profile Books Ltd
29 Cloth Fair
London
EC1A 7JQ

www.serpentstail.com

Copyright © Adrian Duncan, 2025

1 3 5 7 9 10 8 6 4 2

Typeset in Fournier by MacGuru Ltd
Printed and bound in Great Britain by
CPI Group (UK) Ltd, Croydon CRO 4YY

The moral right of the author has been asserted.

This is a work of fiction. All characters, businesses, organisations,
artworks and events portrayed in this novel are either products
of the author's imagination or are used fictitiously.

A CIP catalogue record for this book is available from the British Library.

ISBN 978 1 80522 194 4
eISBN 978 1 80522 195 1

To my sister Clare

The ruined temple is not merely a wreck on
a sea of forms; it itself is nature ...

Marguerite Yourcenar, from *The Dark Brain of Piranesi*

PART I

ACHIM AND BETTINA

It is ski season in this small city of I_.

As Bernadette and I walk, the mountains around us empty of people while the sky falls from dark navy to blacks. Funiculars and cable cars rush downward, hurtling skiers to a squat building at the end of a broad strip-lit bridge that runs into the belly of the old town. The restaurants on the western side fill, but the centre of the city remains almost motionless.

Bernadette and I venture into the eastern part, street after umbrageous street. It's cold and we've not spoken since we left the apartment half an hour ago, to find at this late hour a portion of warm fondue.

There's a sculpture in a park in the middle of the city, of the Romantic-era poets Achim and Bettina von Arnim. It stands over three metres tall and is cast in a now patina'd bronze. Achim sits, grasping the collar of his jacket, gazing in one direction, while Bettina, sitting and leaning back onto his chest, is looking in another. Bernadette and I have spent our time here in I_ drawing, measuring, photographing and studying this sculpture in an attempt to better understand its form.

Through a fall of snow, Bernadette and I come upon a poorly lit laneway, framing, at its end, brightness. As we go, I tell Bernadette about an image that of late has come persistently to mind. It is of the gable of my parents' white bungalow where we lived when I was a boy, and this abode sits a field beyond a creosoted fence behind which I stand while looking on guilelessly at this gable, my heart thumping, waiting for any sign of life.

Bernadette asks me where this bungalow is now.

'It was demolished,' I say, 'years ago ... to make room for an expanding limestone quarry in which my father once worked.'

We descend a tree-lined street that opens onto a park flanked to the right by a ridge, stepped out in timber seating. The ridge arcs down to a frozen pond with patches of snow cast across its surface like handfuls of seed. White poplars sway on another hill beyond the pond, and these leaning trees encased in the darkness seem to draw up into them the last of the receding snow.

Along the pond's edge, we approach a lamp standing in its own cone-throw of light. We climb broad steps up into a dark garden maze, crowded around by manicured trees of hovering shapes – cubes, pyramids, spheres. Then we climb a parting set of steps topped with statues ushering us – snow glistening on their fingers and arms – towards lawns and shrubs that funnel down between two arrowing lengths of wall to a cobblestoned square with an ornate lantern hanging from the corner of a restaurant and swaying wantonly in the breeze.

I wake in the night to the dark. My stomach churns.

In the hallway of our rental I meet Bernadette passing me half asleep and entering her bedroom.

I bend over the toilet and throw up only bile, and realise as I ease my fingers further down my throat that to throw up such a mass of fondue and bread might cause pain.

I fill a glass of water and return to my bed, look at my Nokia and note that I have three hours of rest until six o'clock. I lie there and listen; then, I close my eyes and wait for sleep, but it comes only in fits and, in what feels like minutes, Bernadette is at my door, smiling, clothed for the outdoors and telling me that it's time to rise.

'*Caffè*?' she asks.

The first time I heard tell of Bernadette was in an email I received almost three years ago from an Italian curator called Filippo Conte. In the subject line were these strange words, barely a question: *What is it they can see?*

Filippo told me that he and a team of two other visual-art curators were embarking on an EU-funded project to compile a 'history from within' of a selection of sculptures spread across the European mainland. He told me he wanted to work with 'non-artists' and that he'd come across some of my writing on an English website devoted to stone restoration and for which I'd written about three projects I'd worked on in recent years. Filippo said that he found it interesting the way in which I speculated in these articles about the whole form of the ruined edifice, by basing its extensions upon 'the negative space of what remained'. He said that he enjoyed how I likened this act of visualisation to the act of drawing. He then told me that he hoped to pair me with an Italian sociologist called Bernadette Basagni, and he included an essay of hers on the work of August Comte where she considered what his ideals of Order and Progress might mean for a sociologist today. I was informed that this project was one of several other curatorial engagements that Filippo was concerned with at the time and that this one could last, on and off, for a few years. He told me that it would involve some travel. I'd returned from the east coast of the United States after over a decade of working on building sites there and had set myself up as a consultant for public restorations. During the last few years in the US I'd apprenticed as a carpenter, and I was keen to return to working with the material

I first trained in, during my twenties – stone – so I registered as a small business, took out insurance and began tendering for the overseeing of small restorations as a subcontractor to the Board of Works. These sites were often located in fields far from public roads and in the more forgotten parts of rural Ireland, and when Filippo contacted me I was finishing up my current projects with no new ones on the horizon, so I emailed him back to say I'd give his proposal a go. He asked me if I could be in Athens in a month's time, to which I said, 'Of course.'

Bernadette and I turn down a cobbled dawn-blue street, walking at pace now until we enter the park where Achim and Bettina sit in the centre of an oval of flickering street lights.

Bernadette arranges her tripod and camera, and after some rearranging and tweaking, she directs the lens towards the sculpture and pulls focus.

I remove several large sheets of paper from my roll. Then, I smoothen them out into a folder we've fashioned from plywood and fabric.

A mountain bird calls, and in the distance a light pings on, brightening a carriage at the base of a funicular. A car passes some streets behind, then the rattle of a rubbish truck. The funicular carriage ascends. As Bernadette blows onto her fingers, the camera's screen comes up and her large blue eyes turn green as she scans it. She purses her lips and with this appear the dimples in her cheeks.

'*Fatto*,' she says, as she hits record on her camera.

While we sit on a park bench with the camera recording the light falling across the sculpture's surface, Bernadette produces in her notebook drawing after expert drawing of Achim and Bettina – a nose, a hand meeting a forearm, an eye, a cheek, an ear. She tells me about the year she spent in art college when she was young and how she found what the place did to her curiosity unsettling. She reckons that the world, if she stayed working as an artist, would be reduced to mere raw material for her work, and instead of pursuing ideas to the point where her curiosity was exhausted, these

9

fascinations would be pursued only to where they would be applicable to her art, and then this curiosity 'would fall out of use', she claims. 'And that is why I left,' she says. She then tells me about a happy Erasmus year she spent studying sociology in Glasgow. Then she turns to me, pushing some strands of her frizzy auburn hair off her brow, and utters in a broad Scottish brogue, 'Awright, pal?!'

She draws in pencil – a soft and stubby 4B. When I first trained as a restorative sculptor, I was taught to draw with a pen using cross-hatching and line to model space and volume. Yesterday, while we sat drawing the other side of the sculpture, she took the pen out of my hand and gave me her pencil and asked me to try it instead, but once I directed the tip to my paper, she took the pencil from between my forefinger and thumb and put it sidelong between my thumb and the undersides of my four fingers. Then she gently twisted my palm over until my knuckles faced me. She took my down-turned hand in hers and, with the side of the pencil lead, she had me score out a series of short curves, then she asked me to look at the tone along and across the curves themselves. 'You should try drawing like this,' she said; 'it'll give you more light and shadow, and when the drawing departs from what you're trying to capture,' she said, 'lines like this will help the drawing find its own form.'

Bernadette and I pack away the camera, and with our flapping sheets of paper in hand we approach Achim and Bettina to rub and record the surface markings.

The local office of public works here told us that the sculpture was gifted to them in the winter of 1986 by the city of Warsaw. It was cast there some years before by a now apparently defunct Soviet-era collective, whose name we are as yet unable to find. I picture this cumbersome object being dangled into position, on a winter's morning, from a crane surrounded by council workers from whose mouths issue billowing puffs of breath.

I step – quiet clangs at my feet – up onto the sculpture and drape my sheet of paper over Bettina's thigh. Bernadette climbs high onto Achim's shoulder, drapes her sheet of paper over his crown and records the surface of his head, down past his eyes, his lips, his ears, his cheeks.

We work like this for hours, stepping from and back up onto the object, carefully rubbing, lifting and building an archive of the surface, with which we aim to make to-scale plaster models. People pass by; some ask what we are doing, then smile vaguely and gaze past us when we begin to explain. As Bernadette works, she sometimes gathers her hair over a shoulder, revealing the side of her face, her jaw, the pale nape of her neck. Whenever she returns to the plywood sleeve to number then place her sheet on top of mine, she looks over my work – not with any admiration but more in the way of an auditor reviewing the file of a person new to a company. Then she places her sheet down and closes the sleeve again.

After dark, when Bernadette and I return with our implements to our apartment, I prepare a meal of tuna pasta and warm bread rolls. Bernadette charges the batteries of her camera and begins to play back the footage of the sculpture at dawn, now enlarged tenfold on the box TV perched on the sitting-room dresser. As we eat, we watch Achim and Bettina come to light.

But while the object emerges on the screen, I feel myself with almost equal slowness slump on the couch to sleep, until the last thing I think I see is Bernadette's lovely face looking down at me, her brow knotted in curiosity and her left hand now resting gently on my chest.

2

KRITIOS BOY

Out of my living-room window stands an empty building site, behind which the morning sun rises. This frame of concrete was to be another stubby tower of apartments, built to mirror the crumbling luxury block I live in now, but, as the building rose, there emerged pyrites problems in the soil of that site and in all of the sites to the north, onto which now slump scores of new but derelict houses. I bought my apartment off the plans some years back, with money I'd made while at first labouring for about six years on a variety of sites in the suburbs of Baltimore, then working as an apprentice carpenter in Philadelphia for a few more. The day I moved in here, the whole place was empty, and as far as I can tell, nobody lives on the upper floors still, and yet at night comes the gentle cranking of the lift up and down its shaft. I once asked the owner of this building why my block did not fall asunder too and he told me that apparently they used a superior type of gravel as fill for underneath the foundations, and this did not trigger the destructive reactions and expansions in the soil, like elsewhere.

The floor-to-ceiling corner window of my apartment looks out over this wasteland, so instead of using this living space for relaxing in, I decided to convert it into a studio of sorts, with three trestle worktops: a wet table, where I cast small plaster and silicon models of the ruins I work on from month to month; then, to its right, a dry table, with samples of stone alongside a row of chisels. It is here I produce small carvings and patterns on the faces of this variety of stone that I have found in the ruins down the country. The patterns I sculpt sometimes extend into simple figurative bas reliefs, of which many are left unfinished. And then, to the right, I've placed a research table covered over now in paper and small squares of card onto which I have recently begun composing a taxonomy of stone based on samples from a region in the midlands, near to where I was born, but where I am these days engaged in the restoration of an ancient church ruin. This taxonomy of rocks sits under the heading *Strength Recognition and Description*, and I'm trying to arrange them from Very Strong Rock (granites and marbles) with compressive strengths of over thirty thousand pounds per square inch, which requires 'firm hammering to break', down to the no-man's-land between Very Weak Rock and Very Stiff Soil, which seem to have a compressive strength of a mere forty pounds per square inch. In my descriptions of this material I say that it can be 'broken by hand' or even 'indented with a fingernail'. A few small samples of clay and stone are arranged upon the table too – paltry grey things that I found at the base of the escarpment running below the church ruin.

Out of some rays of wan sunlight falling across my

left-hand table, I pick up the foot-tall plaster model I cast yesterday of Achim and Bettina. It is beginning to dry out nicely and lighten in tone and weight. It's based on the drawings and markings I recorded with Bernadette back in I_, and yet there is something in the form that does not quite make sense to me.

The first time Bernadette and I met was in a tiny cellar restaurant in central Athens. We were there to convene with the curator, Filippo, who was working on an art biennial. Bernadette and I had been asked to prepare, as part of the biennial's catalogue, an early draft of our texts on the famous figurative sculpture *Kritios Boy*.

I arrived in the restaurant first and met Filippo. The place, pierced with lengths of smoke-filled light, smelt of fresh loaves, fried fish fillets and bubbling chickpea stews. Filippo was seated at the end of a wooden table, beside a plump, bearded man. Filippo greeted me warmly and introduced me to this soft-handed painter whose name I cannot remember – he was a man who showed no interest in me whatsoever, whereas Filippo, in what seemed to me an unsustainable show of attentiveness, told me that he found my writing about restoration 'fascinating'.

Then, at the steps leading down into this small and convivial restaurant, Bernadette appeared. She was wearing navy running shoes and a long dark sleeveless summer dress. Sunshine slanted across her torso. She looked about a while, until Filippo noticed her and waved her over. Then he introduced us all.

Kritios Boy is an ancient Greek sculpture of a youth hesitating, but it is now damaged, armless and legless from his shins down. What's left of him is installed on a raised metal plinth in the Acropolis Museum. He gestures all day at nothing. His hollowed white-marble head and blank eyes stare out across a suspended landscape of other frozen and ancient figures.

He's in proportion, but is only two thirds the scale of a human youth. There's this naturalistic swivel in his hips that is thought to be the first instance in sculpture where motion was successfully suggested. The art historians refer to it as a moment of 'contrapposto' – counterpoise, where the figure stands with most of its weight on one foot. It seemed to me, when I first saw him, as if he were magically about to step towards someone or something that had caught his eye. I sat for an age looking at him and trying to complete the shape of his long-gone arms and to where they might have been gesturing, or whom they were hoping to embrace, but there was not form or source material enough for me to find sufficient footing for my imaginings. Bernadette was alongside me all that week, drawing incessantly his face, his gently expanded ribcage – as if on the edge of breath – and his damaged right knee hovering above an absent shin. It was as if these three elements of his body were portals into the mystery of this form, his view of the Earth, and the distant thoughts of his maker.

Some months after all of this, Bernadette produced her catalogue text on *Kritios Boy*. It consisted of fragments describing the day in 1886 when his head was finally unearthed by

German archaeologists. She brought to life the moment when the veil of soil was first pulled back from his eyes, and how the light and the strange men's faces filled his field of vision as his long-detached head was lifted free of the dirt. My text described what he heard and saw two thousand years earlier, moments before his head was toppled from his body – phantoms, caprices, rising up into the air around him in chaotic displays, showing the conflagration and sacking of Athens. After we finished this project, but before we were asked to begin on Achim and Bettina, Bernadette emailed me out of the blue late one evening to tell me how much she liked my description and my observation, near the end of the text, where I said that *Kritios Boy* was probably, in this reconstituted form, homesick.

It is some days later and from my desk I can see the evening sun is now descending outside, throwing the gnarled shadow of my neighbouring tower block across the puddles and surrounding soil. I close my laptop and turn off my kitchen light. Then, flicking on some anglepoise lamps, I sit at my second table, which is covered over in drawings of caryatids I traced from an encyclopaedia some years ago. I've begun to carve in miniature the caryatid stolen by Lord Elgin; I'm using a piece of sandstone I found one day on this same site in the midlands, this church for a bygone brotherhood of priests. In preparation, this lump of sandstone was shorn down with broad chisel strokes to a foot-high and a half-foot-wide cuboid of stone. Then, with red chalk, I drew onto the four faces of the piece of stone the outline of this strange quiet-eyed column-being. In the last few days I've begun with a small claw chisel to delve beyond the planar faces to find the curves and the form within. As I go, tapping the back of my chisel and carving further into the stone, I find the chalk lines on the surface, which at first guided me, begin to disappear and I am left to negotiate the stone and the potential forms within in a colourless darkness of my own. As different features and folds appear, my mind turns into that of a kind of hunter, but one whose quarry is the good trapping of shadow. When I am in a flow with tool tip upon grain of stone, I realise that there are no mistakes in work of this kind, only other avenues of approach. Then, I find often, while working on an object and apprehending the perfect shadow, my sense of time disappears into the whole activity and, when I come to my senses again, it is often deep into the small hours of the night.

More recently, in quiet times like these, standing back and looking at these chess-piece-like objects across my tables, and when the adrenaline from my day has fully fallen away, I begin to see in my mind's eye, ghosting *Kritios Boy*'s ruins of a flaming Athens, the gable of my parents' bungalow from almost forty years ago. I think sometimes one sight has begun to happily coax the other into being. I've been visited by these sorts of daydreams since my youth and from where these vivid sights come or go I do not know, but I do know that my parents' bungalow always arrives with the faint smell of creosote and is usually motionless except for the rustle of grass in the foreground, the heaving of a stand of chestnut trees framing out the distance and the cavalier sailing of a crow through the air, before it descends onto an electricity wire drooping from the apex of the bungalow down to a water-stained pole at the side of the roadway below.

Then, on nights after the most florid or most convincing of visions, I wake in the dark with the rock-like rind of my consciousness loosened and breached, and into this flows, through the stone citadel of my person, not further images but flood-like – image-decimating – feelings of guilt. It is as if this terrain around me is at last showing itself to be made up of an ancient if poorly conceived complex of civil works, unable to handle these incursions from the water table below.

Igneous rock I: Basalt
Grain size: fine
Main minerals: feldspar, mafic
Structure: sheet
Strength: strong
Breaking pattern: colonnade, columnar

It's a week or so later, just after midnight, and while I try to picture Bernadette and what she might now be doing, I take a seat at my research table, across which I've just spread a range of photographs I once took of a tiny sculpture by a nineteenth-century Irish artist called Launt Thompson.

It was when I was in my mid-thirties, some years after I'd finished studying restorative sculpture in Utrecht, that I first saw, in the flesh, the work of Thompson. It was the week around Labour Day and I was on a six-day break from my work labouring on timber-frame houses in the suburbs of Philadelphia, and I had a strange longing for stone, so I took a drive up and down the east coast, from Philadelphia to Boston and back, and while on this trip I decided to visit the Albany Institute in Washington. I saw Thompson's *Unconsciousness* there, one of the few uncommissioned sculptures he made during his career. I'd learned from old art-history books that he'd sculpted mostly military memorials, so I was always interested in how a work he made out of a pure devotion to his craft might look. The evening before, I'd seen his remarkable, if dejected, *Napoleon the First* at the Smithsonian Mall, and I felt like I had a good handle on his at once academic and intuitive style. *Unconsciousness* is a small reclining female nude Thompson sculpted when he lived in Florence. The card next to this white-marble work – it was sitting alone in a glass cabinet in a large and well-lit room to the rear of the Albany – told me that its other title was *The Chief's Bride* and that the figure depicted was a young 'settler' woman, who as a girl had been 'kidnapped by Native Americans', but on reaching adulthood she was offered by the chief of the tribe the choice of returning to her fellow settlers or taking his hand in marriage. She chose to marry, and this piece depicts her playing absentmindedly with a baby turtle, which the plaque went on to inform me was supposedly a symbol of this tribe. The funny thing was that I'd interpreted her posture as a pensive kind of waiting in that in-between moment of her wedding night, and I read the turtle as her merely toying with the end of her childhood.

I turn the lamps on my desk off and, as I stand to return to my kitchen to shut down my laptop and go to bed, I hear an incoming email ping. It's from Bernadette and she is arranging our return trip to I_.

In the PS after her initials – *BB* – she tells me that she read, an evening or two before, that in ancient Greece, if a statue fell on you, any damage it caused was considered to be the responsibility of the statue.

When did we stop believing in the life in motionless things? she asks.

Then, some minutes later, she emails me, asking if I was shy when I was young.

Weren't all young boys shy? I write, but there comes no response.

3

SANDRA

My train creaks then swerves towards the snow-topped mountains in the distance. I am to arrive in I_ in an hour or so, where Bernadette awaits.

The dining car, filled with passengers, shudders as I take a sip from my *Weissbier*. Around me up-thrusts of rock and ice and stands of trees emerge out of the land.

We clatter into darkness, and I can feel the train slowing into a dip; then we accelerate out of the mountain and into the gleaming upper climes of the Alps, which carve out the sky above.

These drifting clouds, clumps of evergreens and the snow enveloping the train as it drives onward, become, to a lowland sort like me, exhilarating.

The train shakes once more, and from a carriage behind, a metallic clank grows into a rhythmic boom. I peer out the window, looking back at the far end of the train following itself along the curve as we climb. More snow dashes against the walls and swirls across the carriage roof, as the windows either side cloud over.

Each year, when I was young, a rich local landowner held an international hot-air balloon race a few towns to the east of ours. The prevailing wind was from the south-west, so we, in this town west of the balloon race, rarely ever saw these balloons. It was as if the event took place in a distant or fictional county.

One summer's evening, as my mother and I drove from my football practice back to our bungalow, I remember seeing in the sky above, floating around like unmoored coordinates, hot-air balloons racing on what must have been an easterly breeze. I imagined the curved spaces created between them up there as cool, airless, holy.

When we got home, there was a note on the kitchen table saying that my uncle had called and picked up my father to drive him to a field nearby where one of these balloons had supposedly crash landed. My mother and I went to join them.

As I chased across the field, I could see the fallen balloon, which looked like a giant stricken animal being resuscitated. The wicker basket had toppled onto its side, with a pointed flame sending hot air back into this exhausted form. I walked around it and found two men hunkered at the other end, repairing a strip of rubber. They told me they were going to 'lift off again'. I stalked around the flailing thing once more, until, on one flank, with no one there to see me, I stepped forward and touched it. I stepped back to see how or if my gesture had altered anything. Then I pushed again – harder, this time – on the flank of this creature, until a dried cow pat was revealed in the bent grass below. The ease with which I put this huge object out of shape, and the feeling on the palm of my hand at that time, touching this angelic thing, is one I can still feel if I close my eyes and think back to the hollow roar of a gas flame, the smell of silage, dung, and the excited murmurs of those ghostly figures gathering round. By the time I returned to the wicker basket, the balloon was beginning to lift from the ground like a person's head, still heavy with sleep, rising from their pillow at dawn. Two men and a woman struggled to hold the wicker basket at an angle as the aviators – or 'continental ballooning enthusiasts', as my mother called them – arranged themselves within to direct the blue jets of hot air into the anus of the bloating beast. I remember my father leaning on his walking stick, his older and yet far healthier brother beside him, both of them looking up at this tear-like balloon taking shape above the broad green field. My mother joined them. She took my father's hand in hers and squeezed, and he looked to her and smiled. Then they both squinted up at the balloon now stretching skyward. I looked down at the base of the wicker basket to see that instant when it lifted free, and, when it did, I saw many blades of longer grass caught in the folds and weft of the wicker tug for a moment, until they were overwhelmed.

Bernadette's eyelids quake as she peers into the mountain wind. She leans in against me as we look on at the swooping and disappearing of a dozen or so calling birds. Other visitors in colourful hats and scarfs drift to and from this viewpoint that looks down onto the city of I_. As I approach the stone parapet – and as the air expands – I feel an intense triangulating tingle in the centre of my stomach. I step back as two birds, as if on wires, swing past and away. They cascade down into the valley below, then career again up on a contour of air.

We try to make out the park far below where Achim and Bettina now sit, but we cannot see a thing. Bernadette shrugs and suggests to me I follow her.

She makes off towards a path leading to a blowy upper flank, over which a light snow now scatters.

As we go, the path narrows and the folds of land to the right fall away.

Eye-high clouds scud past, as Bernadette walks on hymning a light-hearted tune, but I begin to falter.

'I want to show you some goats!' she calls over her shoulder. 'Down in the city, I was told that there are ibex up here!'

Through the twilight, we descend in the cable car, back towards the base of the mountain.

As we judder past a support, and then, for a second, soar, Bernadette takes hold of my hand.

It's warm and encompassing.

She squeezes, and I squeeze back.

Through the snow-lined trees, we see an old restaurant between the foothills of the mountain and the edge of the city beyond.

We find two seats at the bar and order a glass each of a local beer.

An old moustachioed man appears from behind the bar, looks around the otherwise empty room and goes.

A clock ticks through an open door.

Bernadette and I sit for a while in a strange shyness into which we say very little.

Then she asks me about family and my home.

So, I tell Bernadette about the winter night when my mother, Sandra, saw a statue of the Virgin Mary speaking to her in a grotto to the rear of a country church a mile outside of our town.

'It was the last day of January in 1972,' I say, 'and it happened long before such things were in vogue. I was only nine years old at the time.'

And I then recall to Bernadette the beatific, absent smile on my mother's face when she arrived home that night, her clothes soaked through to her glowing skin.

I tell Bernadette that I found it terrifying to see my mother, all of a sudden, at once so elated and so reduced.

Bernadette looks at me a while, but says nothing.

'Languageless but beautiful, was how she described it,' I say to Bernadette.

Then, I tell her about how my mother was asked by the local priest to check herself into a psychiatric hospital in Dublin for a month, to 'get over these hallucinations', as he called them. I then tell her that I've not spoken about this to anyone before. And as I sip my beer in this old bar, I picture that adamant bald priest at the head of my old classroom with a blackboard behind him filled with lists showing the hierarchy of saints' names, he on one of his regular visits, teaching us boys the catechism.

'He insisted that she go,' I say, putting my glass back down onto the bar, 'out of form.'

'And did you believe her?' asks Bernadette.

'It never occurred to me not to,' I reply. '... And we visited her for weeks, my father and I, in that dreadful hospital in a dark corner of Dublin, bringing her sweets and flowers, and watching her change. Then one night some weeks later,' I say, taking a sip from my beer, 'my father received a beating when he'd defended her honour in our local pub. A few over-devout young men had called my mother a heathen for "adoring the false god of the Virgin Mother". The beating broke him, though,' I say to Bernadette, 'and not because of the injuries that wrecked his balance forever, or because these men were once school friends of his, but because it made clear to him that he, my mother and I were now outsiders in the town. He never fully recovered his sense of balance, and this led,' I say, 'to accidents at the quarry where he worked and forced him into early retirement, until he passed away when I was eighteen.'

Bernadette raises an eyebrow. Then, looking at me, her eyes softening, she gives my arm a rub.

'It's gas,' I say. 'About ten years later, the whole blooming country was seeing statues of the Virgin Mother, all over the place, moving and speaking!

'But they weren't hallucinations – "Marian Apparitions", was how they classed it,' I say.

Then, after a silence filled with the weekday quiet of the bar, Bernadette turns to me and begins to gather up her hair, and she smiles and tells me about when she was young, and the variety of absurd hairstyles she had through her teens, laughing at herself at times, and she then points out a small impression on her nose where she had it pierced with a ring. She tells me she was a punk and a tearaway and, growing up, had countless run-ins with her mother. Then she tells me how she met her ex-husband, Stefano. It was at a music festival near Pisa and he was camping in a tent next to hers, and they simply began talking.

'Simple as all that,' she says, dusting her palms.

I take a sip from what's left of my beer as she plays for a moment with the black onyx ring on her forefinger. Then she lifts her large fabric bag from the bar and, from a side pocket, she takes out a photograph of her eight-year-old daughter, Philomena. She looks at me and back to the photograph, telling me that Philomena has her father's dark eyes but, unfortunately for her, her mother's hot temperament ... and at this she laughs once more.

Stone, like glass, is strong when compressed, but is quite fragile and prone to rupture when pulled apart or suddenly struck. A stone carver, then, is a rupturer of stone, and a restorative stone carver is at first an embalmer and then an enhancer of this initial pattern of rupture. Over the years, I have come to enjoy working with granite most, because I can tell from the grain in a piece of granite the way it formed on cooling, epochs ago, and if I can tell this, then I can imagine the molten igneous flows before this cooling took hold. Granite normally gives good strength in one direction, but, if the rift plane of the stone was more complex or formed in other directions too, then the grain in the stone becomes less uniform, and, though a more complex stone like this may be much easier to quarry, it is more difficult to sculpt.

Over our last lovely day in I_, Bernadette and I walked around the city taking pictures and making drawings of the strange rock that we realised was used in almost all the walls of the city's buildings. We stopped into a bookshop café for refreshments and we asked the owner about this rock. Her face brightened as she told us it was called *Höttinger Brekzie*, a limestone mined on the other side of the northern ridge, and she gestured out the window, to beyond the wet street flanked with grey pointed roofs, and on up to the white mountain peaks floating amid the clouds far above. The stone's surface seemed so porous and grainless, and I imagined, as Bernadette and I walked around looking at it and rubbing it, that if I were to strike it with a pointed chisel this matrix of aggregates and clastic sediment would fall apart in directions I could never foresee. I then imagined every ounce of this rock transforming itself into currents of silt-laden water, and all of the city of I_ lying underwater too, with only its arches and walls and lintels and towers discernible through the slower-moving silt drawing out its forms within its fluid world. I imagined walking with Bernadette through these quiet sub-aquatic streets of an underwater I_ and coming upon not Achim and Bettina, in their romantic pose, but instead a statue of a lost Greek caryatid looking on impassively at this glittering architecture of silt gathering and dispersing around her, and it struck me that, whenever I look at a figurative sculpture in this world, that the object at hand must, like this, be enveloped in a medium of its own, which I myself can scarcely or will never wholly penetrate.

Then, near the end of that last day together in I_, Bernadette suggested we swap the notebooks we'd been keeping while taking our measures of Achim and Bettina. She wanted to see where our thoughts were going. As I flicked through her notebook, taking in her small sketches and doodles and notes in Italian, with arrows to and from one thing to another and another – sometimes pages apart – inventing for her connections and new routes of enquiry, I saw, among three rough sketches of Bettina's hands, a tiny drawing of my face in profile.

It is some weeks later, evening, and the land outside is dark. The city twinkles in the distance, its lines of electric light crisscrossing the vague reflection of me in the window, seated and hovering out beyond. It is during late hours like these, on weekdays like this, when my apartment block is at its most silent.

I'm sitting once more at my research table, clearing away my old photos of Thompson's *Unconsciousness* and placing on the table instead the cards showing my unfinished taxonomy of stone. I'm struggling to find descriptions for the way one might break open the middle-strength stones on my list – the sandstones and shales. I've tried such formulations as *Can be broken by hammer in hand*, but I am unsure if this might read as the stone in hand or the hammer in hand, or both. I'm considering *Can be dented with chisel* or perhaps even *Cannot be cut with a saw*. I wonder then if I ought to include how the rock responds to these blows, with descriptions like *Crumbles under blow from hammer* or *Mostly retains form, but cleaves under blow from pointed chisel*. I've written them out on these pieces of card and put them next to a list of rock types, from granite, marble and basalt on through to limestone, sandstone and into the clays. I've begun to realise that I'd like to extend my project beyond stones found around sites in the midlands and produce instead an atlas that connects the most famous incidents of sculpted stone back to the parts of the Earth's crust from where they were mined, and from this I'd like to include a lithospheric description of the most recent geological processes that brought that seam of rock into place. This might then show a reader something of the stone and the conditions encountered by the sculptor while the object in question was being shaped.

I bring an unruly lump of limestone in under the light of my lamps and lift a small, pointed axe, and I administer to the stone a slight sidelong smack to see what's just beneath the skin. I lift the shining stone closer to my eyes, then back, and I strike it once more, and again, and again, and as if like sparks from a flint, an image comes to mind of my mother – from that night, decades ago – of her shivering on our sitting-room floor, holding herself and grimacing in goose-pimpled ecstasy, and I realise when I see this image again and again and again ... that I've not thought fairly about my mother for years. I realise that, when she fell into the habit of praying, she eroded the selvedges of her consciousness and this must have led to these incursions and visions and religious experiences. I realise also that, when she accepted what she saw in that grotto that night, years ago, she must have felt a kind of collegiality with these holy entities, and then afterwards she must surely have felt an abandonment from them that neither my father nor I could have allayed.

Even though she was in and out of hospital often, then, we still had some great weeks together. Some days, when I'd arrive in from school, she would pretend for the evening that she was a cat, a wolf, a cow, and we would not speak a word of English until the following morning, and, with my father already gone to work at the quarry beyond the hill, she'd appear in my room and almost sheepishly help me get ready for school. Then there were other evenings that were far less carefree, and she'd fall deeply into herself, her intelligent dark eyes glazing over while looking at once at me and right through me. Mostly, I assumed, from the savage grinding of her teeth, she was lost somewhere else far away from me, in prayer. I remember on one such day, when I was maybe eleven or so, she told me that, when you are being haunted, you are not seeing some strange otherworldly entity, some ghost appear before you, but it is more that the haunting entity has entered your person, to the point that you begin to see what this entity sees ... 'And when you are being haunted, John,' she said, my hand in hers, 'you are not looking at strange things in your world, but actual things before the eyes of the haunter.'

I did not sleep for weeks.

By my early twenties, she was mostly in care, and I used to travel up each weekend from my home town to see her. It always seemed to me that she, by this time, could not wait to leave this planet that had taken and disintegrated her 'dear Tom Molloy'. Whenever I visited her, she was heavily sedated, and I found it hard to watch her even more leadened to this world and its banal old gravity that, in some deep part of her, she clearly wished to be free of.

Then, near the end, on the late buses home on Sunday nights, looking out at the gleaming fields and the glittering pub-filled towns passing quietly outside, I remember resolving to turn myself away from her impossible sky and look instead to the rocks and tides of the Earth. And yet, these days, decades later, I feel myself turning back again to look once more at what might have been her sky.

Earlier this afternoon, I visited that church in the midlands to cast an eye over the pointing work that had been carried out on the south-facing wall.

The land, mostly rolling countryside, was developing along its hedges and fallow fields the faintest hue of spring-time green. I turned my van up into a gravel laneway halfway up a hill, and in the rear-view mirror I could see the rising dust. The grass surrounding the graves in the churchyard had recently been snipped back, most likely by the caretaker, an old man with large hands who has come and gone silently during my time here.

I stepped around the church, and approached the western gable. Here, the ground rose towards the boundary wall, before falling away again, but over many miles of empty fields, where it opened out into a distant and serene-seeming lake, across which a rowing boat barely moved. A bird lifted weightily from the shore, while another veered in to land. Five swifts descended on a broad tree in the shape of a brain. The wind blew into my face as ravens cawed overhead, while cows, as the breeze picked up, chased off across the next field, and then, from this unruly boundary hedge emerged a giant man controlling a huge charging bull, both covered in fluttering ivy.

I turned and rounded the flank of the church and stepped inside, and there, leaning against a bramble-covered wall to the rear, I saw a pristine Marian-year statue of the Virgin Mary. I stood for some moments staring at this object, and I considered lifting it and returning it to the front wall so as to make the caretaker of the cemetery aware of its presence, but it occurred to me that it was perhaps he who had left it here for safekeeping. I looked on a moment at the Virgin Mother's eyes cast so earnestly skyward. Then, I gathered up what remained of my tapes and tools, and left.

While the sun was setting this evening, I sat at my second table and took to chiselling and rasping away on the emerging arms and torso of my small stone carving of Elgin's caryatid. I was too tired to take on the distant expression in her face.

Then, hours later, I woke with my head resting on the table and with the caryatid now almost done.

4

THE OLD WALLED TOWN OF FERRARA

I finished up work today on that once-crumbling church in the midlands. Then, I drove back to my apartment and, while having a few beers, my old friend Anna called and we spoke for some time on the phone.

Anna runs a number of complicated restorations in towns dotted around the south and west. We call each other often if we need a 'dig out' or some advice. She's a stocky woman with short dark hair and squinting blue eyes. She has what I'd call a gentle inner power to her. She's been kind to me ever since we met, and, because I don't have siblings, I often think of her as an older and wiser sister. And whenever, over the years, I've felt myself drifting away from myself, I've often called down to one of her restorations to see her. And she, I assume, began to understand, in the lack of any reason for my visit, that all I wanted was to be near her for a bit.

As I finish up my last beer and stand to boil the kettle for a peppermint tea to settle my stomach before I go to bed, my Nokia buzzes into life.

It's a message from Bernadette asking me if I might ever like to meet her again.

Bernadette, walking through a shaft of afternoon sun, removes her red cardigan and, folding it into her shoulder bag, tells me that this weekend, if he were still around, would be her father's birthday.

His name was Fernand, and she tells me that he moved to Bologna from Brennero after the war. 'He and my mother, Margaret, were fair-skinned,' she says, squinting into the sun. 'He looked "Tyrolean", as they used to say, and after a while our neighbours began calling them "the Tedeschi", the Germans,' she says, as she returns her bag strap to her shoulder.

Then she tells me he worked as a mechanic, but died when she was four in an accident during a car race – a bend taken too quickly.

'My mother didn't remarry,' she says, looking downward as we walk by the winding red walls and the cobbled streets of central Ferrara. 'I inherited his colouring and freckles, though, and my older sister, Louisa, got the hazel in his eyes.'

Then she pulls from her purse a well-thumbed square photograph of him, goggled and smiling proudly, beside a white coupé parked in front of a busy hillside hostelry called Bar Americano. His arms are spread and his mouth is open wide, as if he is singing.

During breakfast this morning, the owner of our guest house – a floppy-haired man in his forties, called Franco – told us that today was a big one for the town and its football club.

'We are to play a southern giant,' he said to me in his accented English, 'but the Roman mafia, they will get to the referee and see to it we lose – wait till you see!'

He was standing in his dining room at the time, a blue-and-white Ferrara flag slung over his shoulders. In his outstretched hands draped a banner with the words *FERRARA NEL CUORE* – Ferrara in my heart – emblazoned across it in crimson cursive.

In a corner shop two streets from the guest house, Bernadette and I procure from the owner touted tickets for the match.

As we leave, I tell Bernadette that I played football when I was young, but that I've not looked at a game for years, and I recall to her the day when I was sixteen and playing for my local team and the bone between my knee and ankle was snapped in two.

'It was a tackle on the opposition's midfielder,' I say, 'a stout lad for his age. He was the eldest son of one of the men who had beaten my father, and I suppose I was seeking revenge … I collapsed,' I say to Bernadette. 'Then, I tried to sit up and slot the lower part of my leg back in line with my shin.'

'Then, darkness.'

Bernadette winces and shakes out a hand as we round a corner into a narrow voice-filled street leading us away from the foothills of the cathedral, whose bells have begun to dong, shivering the air, and then she asks me if this injury ever troubles me now.

'Not at all,' I say.

Supporters, draped in blue and white, converge at street corners – singing, embracing and drinking.

A cycling race passes. Pink-hatted columns of men with enormous thighs fizz in and out of shadows down the main street on their way north to Padua.

Bernadette and I wander through the moated castle in the middle of town and take in the collection of old oil paintings depicting bejewelled and feathered local patrons. Then, as we walk around its quiet rooms and halls, she tells me that she has since found the name of the lead sculptor of Achim and Bettina – a man called Schmid, who has renamed and moved his studio to another part of Warsaw, but exactly where she does not yet know.

'Should we not go sometime?' she asks.

To which I look to her and say that I'd very much like to.

As we leave the castle and rejoin the town, she begins to tell me about a protest she once saw when she was very young, near her parents' apartment in central Bologna, where a piazza statue of the inventor Galvani had tins of red paint and hundreds of fake frogs' legs thrown over it by a group of protesters. She says to me that she believes it is one of her earliest memories and that, at the time, she was with her father's brother, Alfredo, who was part of the Arte Povera movement taking shape in northern Italy then, and she tells me that Alfredo, incensed, stepped towards this horde of protesters who had lost the run of themselves, and he demanded they cease this act of vandalism.

'"What has Galvani ever done to you?" he shouted.

'Then, one of these students threw red paint over my

uncle,' she says, 'and he had to be held back. I was only five or so, but I remember the fight, and especially, after the crowd cleared off, my uncle looking for me frantically. All I could see in the square then was the statue of Galvani up high and my poor bald uncle Alfredo below, both of them draped in slicks of red paint.' Then she tells me about Alfredo's work, all small angular objects made from scraps of material he searched for in skips beside building sites. 'Small and beautiful things,' she says, twisting her hands before her.

As we traverse a broad piazza filled with children and parents flying kites, Bernadette begins to tell me about her work and how her weekly hours of teaching English at her local college in Bologna have been reduced and that she is considering going back to university to begin a PhD in sociology. 'I'd like to study,' she says, her hands now falling open, 'the cultural conditions that embalmed Bologna during the post-war years. And I'd like to do it by looking at civic art commissions from that time.'

After a coffee, we hire bicycles and cycle out and around Ferrara's perimeter wall, looking at the many large flower-filled gaps in the boundary, and as we go I imagine the bricks that once filled these openings are now the makings of some citizen's shed or a small extension elsewhere in the town – a kitchen, perhaps, with a stove in the corner upon which bubbles a pot of water.

The day oscillates from warm to cold to warm, until everything then settles in the late afternoon, when we turn our bicycles for the centre of the town and make off towards the stadium.

While traversing the narrow and busy streets converging on the bowl-shaped stadium in the distance, Bernadette turns to me and asks, as we drift for a moment closer to each other, if it was because of my leg injury that I went on to study stone restoration.

I hesitate as the crowds around us gather, and I can feel her looking at me.

And because this connection between broken bone and stone had not occurred to me before, I just shake my head, and say, 'Don't think so, Bernadette.'

Seething in the southern stand, the hordes of Lazio fans are stripped to their waists and are waving giant blue flags in the evening sun. They chant with a punchy, if almost comical, aggression.

The Ferrara crowd are so good-humoured though, and the volley of singing returned from the large and packed tribune to our left is like a playlist of crooned Italian love songs, all about how much this crowd admire their club, their players and their manager, a small overweight man called Simplici.

Bernadette leans towards me and touches my forearm while she points out a sky-blue-and-white banner unfolding near the top of the home stand. Across it are the words *FERRARA NEL CUORE*. It must be Franco, and in among the giant fluttering flags his banner is minute, but I can imagine him up there beneath it, singing his heart out. He told us earlier – in the morning, while we were finishing our breakfast – about the material he'd used for his banner. As he searched for the word, he drifted towards the dining-room window and took the hem of the curtain in his fingers and uttered the word *reticolato* – netted. And as the morning sunshine broke across him, he explained that, with this material, those behind him would be able to see the game even while he opened out his banner and proclaimed his admiration.

Bernadette gazes on at the swaying fans singing in the distance. Then she turns to me, now smiling widely, and she kisses me on the cheek.

She looks at me a while, her large blue eyes moving over

and back, gauging my response. Then a roar erupts from far across the pitch.

Sometimes, she holds her fist up to her chest and then, when she emphasises something to me, her thumb, forefinger and middle finger spring apart, as if a tiny explosion has propelled her fingertips away in three spirals, until they are halted and the fingers and hand then slump into a gesture that becomes irrelevant to what she has moved on to saying.

I remember, weeks after I snapped my shin, I was told by one of my young teammates that the sound, when the bone broke, was that of a rifle shot.

The piazza shudders.

And what at first felt like a ripple then grows into a roar as flare-wielding hordes pour into the square. From way up on the municipal building behind us comes a high-pitched call as two giant banners unfurl, one with a knight on horseback brandishing a jousting stick and the other showing a dragon with a large red tongue. The people around us jostle and clamour. Bernadette, now speaking loudly to an elderly man a table over, begins to laugh. She tells me this banner depicts Saint George.

On it goes above, this giant painting of Saint George being slid across and back by supporters leaning over the parapet towards the other six, who have unfurled their huge painting of the slayed dragon. It is as if these dozen or so puppet masters have stormed the government buildings of Ferrara to bring news to the piazza below of the great victory claimed in the colosseum outside the city walls.

More red and orange flares pop, smoke billows and, behind these throbbing flares, figures appear, winding through the throngs with drums and trumpets and giant blue-and-white flags, and disappearing into where the shadows grow into darkness and where the whistles trill, the ultras sing and jump in rampant circles, hands in the air, fists pumping, shouts expanding, shivering, receding.

Then, I look over to Bernadette. And she is looking at me.

She puts her hands up to her ears and crosses her eyes, then she nods her head that we should leave. But we are surrounded, so Bernadette stands on a chair and surveys the

53

piazza, looking for a route to escape. She cups her fingers over her brow for a second, as if she is the courageous sea captain of a ship in some peril, facing a hostile incoming armada and deciding how best to organise her ship hands. There is the sound of a distant canon ripping a metal ball into the air, the quiet measuring its distance, before it crashes into the waves half a knot in front of the prow of Bernadette's surging frigate. Netting and sails billow as men clamber up masts, smoke plumes into the air and thousands of lungs of breath back on the mainland are held, and still, she stands, her eyes surveying the approaching bastards, until her shipwright, a toothless and tired man, steps forth to join her at the prow, informing her of the water her ship is taking on, to which she merely nods, accepting that this frigate is now almost useless and doomed to its last voyage, and to this she lets the shipwright on his way and takes her hand from above her brow.

She steps down from the chair and, as another blue-and-white Ferrara flag folds and unfolds expansively in the smoke behind her, she approaches me and whispers into my ear a simple: 'Follow!'

Igneous rock II: Granite
Grain size: fine-to-medium
Main minerals: feldspar, mica, hornblende, quartz
Structure: massive
Strength: very strong (weathers to lower grades)
Breaking pattern: fractal

5

ANNA

Some months have passed since I've seen Bernadette, and weeks since I've heard any word from her. The last email she sent me had a photograph attached, taken by her daughter, Philomena, of Bernadette smiling while eating a pink and blue ice cream at the foot of an old tower made of bricks leaning into the sky.

I go over to my corner window and look out at some workmen in yellow hard hats stomping around the foothills of the tower ruin opposite. One bends to take a photograph, while the other talks into his phone.

Across the surface of my research table are now spread drawings and notes from my years of training in restorative sculpture in Utrecht. Some of the photos show me and Anna beside a half-carved chunk of sandstone – a muscular torso emerging from the guts of the rock. In one of the photos, she is holding her stomach in laughter. I remember, two years into my training, working on a replica of a gargoyle from the eaves of a local Romanesque church. It showed a goat head feasting from a cornucopia disgorging berries and pears. It was such a funny object to replicate, for months on end. I'd place the piece on my circular turntable and then sit alongside it a block of sandstone of similar dimension and, with a stiff old calliper, I'd transfer in red chalk lines the extents of the object I was copying onto the block of sandstone, and, as I rotated both objects, I'd mark what would become the planes of sandstone I could shed from the block, delving closer to the form I was seeking – this goat's twin head within. On this would go for weeks, me mapping with increasing detail the shape, then curvatures and tone of one object onto the emerging features of the other. This was my third sculpture that year and I was becoming adept at replication of this kind, but that first evening, as I looked at the planar shards of sandstone that had toppled over the course of the day to my feet, around this plinth I had been circumnavigating, I realised that these unselfconsciously arranged chunks of stone had a certain ruinous beauty to them. Then, I found that the longer I worked on this sculpture, the more my technique collapsed into a kind of intuition that helped me to foresee problems in the stone, before they even appeared, and then this intuition morphed into a kind of natural improvisation that enabled me to see the whole form emerging from the stone, far beneath the snow storms at my hands of flying fragments and swirls of dust.

I step to my left-hand table and pick up the small statuette of Achim and Bettina. A hairline crack has formed across the base and up over Bettina's shoulder and along her neck and down to where her back meets Achim's chest. The plaster has dried out too much too quickly. I replace the object onto the table and look out my window once more as the men below clear off and a fall of rain surges landward from the coast.

Sometimes, especially in the evenings of late, I find myself trying to picture the view from above my parents' old bungalow. I see the clay roof tiles ripple down to the eaves, around which bloats a driveway of gravel that my father laid with stone bought from the quarry, and surrounding this expands the lush green lawn, dotted out with yellowing shrubs all leading up to a boundary wall, then a water-stained electricity pole, beyond which runs the public road. To the right of this a neighbour has begun clearing the site to begin building their own bungalow. Two tiny barrels, surrounded by planks, stand in the long grass. Our house seems to be empty, and as I look on, the sunlight of this world begins to wane, and the planar shadows lengthen and swing around the building, and soon, as the whole scene becomes dusk, lights come on in the windows and the chimney sends up a climbing string of smoke; then a car slows and turns in from the road, sweeping its headlamps across the front facade of three windows and a door. I look on as the lights in the house begin to go out and the smoke from the chimney thins and disappears into the dark, and I remember the quiet of this two-bedroomed bungalow containing my mother, my father and me, all of us asleep and dreaming into three distant dream worlds connected only by tendrils and desires of that dream day.

The first time I heard the lovely word *feldspar* was one evening when I was six or seven and my father came home from the quarry with a large sample of this pinkish stone in his hands. He brought me to the kitchen table and, pushing his dark curly hair back from his brow, told me, as he manipulated this rock, that he'd found it in the middle of a giant chunk of limestone they'd blown from the quarry face that day. With his little finger, he pointed out to me the rock's *cleavages* and how this rock was once a small crystallising clump of magma. 'Feldspar,' he said, and this word, coming from his lips like this, made it seem to me as if the stone were a small fragment of star that had fallen into a field nearby. He'd often bring home other strange-looking stones with strange-sounding names: *gneiss*, *hornfels*, *schist* … And it seemed at times as if he was bringing home words that just happened to have stones attached to them. Then he'd arrange these multicoloured stones on the small mantelpiece above our sitting-room fire and, every now and then, take one down and, at the kitchen table, with a rag and some sharp-smelling solvents, he'd give it a thorough polish. By the end, the whole mantelpiece was crammed with these ragged shining planets and, in the evenings, I'd often take them down and make small solar systems out of them on the sitting-room floor, solar systems from as yet undetected galaxies that I'd name after townlands in my locale – the galaxy of Derrymór, Derrynagallya, the giant galaxy of Tang – but, of course, I'd never return the stones to the mantelpiece in the way my father had left them, which was left-to-right in the order in which he had found them. This meddling would anger him and he'd chide me firmly, and, by extension of this, chide my mother too, for allowing such chaos to intrude into his order of things, and when he left the room after such chidings my mother would smile to me and say, by way of explanation, 'You know, John, your father is a very simple man in many ways.'

She said this not out of any sense of superiority, but far more so out of feelings of admiration that almost, I realise now, tipped over into feelings of envy.

Then, when he bought his first car, a black second-hand Morris Minor, he'd drive us out into the countryside on Saturday evenings, pointing out erratics on the farmland, and the galaxies I'd imagined on our sitting-room floor extended enormously in scale. 'Great stones dumped there by ancient glaciers,' he'd say. 'Ten storeys of ice moving across the land – can you even imagine the sound of that!'

Today, I began early on a new restoration in a border county. It was once a monastery, and it lies about eighty miles north of the old church I finished up with some months ago. The weather was beautiful, so my fellow restorers and I ended up working for fourteen hours straight, and they, under my direction, shored up several sections of old wall. In one stone in a west-facing wall we found an extremely faint bas relief of a man driving oxen across some fields towards home. It was an amateurish thing, but there was some poetry to it, or perhaps the poetry was in finding it. My journey back to my apartment was long, with much traffic, and by the time I arrived home I was fit only for sleep.

I find, when I begin to think of Bernadette, that the best thing to do is fill the void with work, so I take on any of these small new jobs that I can find.

Sedimentary rock I: Limestone
Grain size: fine
Main minerals: calcite, dolomite
Structure: bedding, lenses, some interbedding
Strength: weak to strong
Breaking pattern: fragmentation

If Bernadette were to one day message me the words: *Do you ever think of me, John?* I would respond with the words: *Often, Bernadette.*

A broad river courses past as it bends away and off through this unruffled corner of County Clare. Above me, clinking scaffolding is being raised to cradle a subsiding gable of an ancient castle. A few fields across from the river stands a roofless Hellfire Club, its walls and crumbling window arches frame slivers of the broad green hills beyond.

My friend Anna, perched high upon the scaffold, shouts an instruction down to a dark-haired junior tradesman called Fatin. She pulls up a tube and clamps it into place, jutting it to the underside of an ancient elbow of stone; then she asks Fatin to join her.

The wind blows up the river again. The reeds bend and return, sending shivers into the water. Anna's and Fatin's hands redden as they criss-cross, lift and tighten these tubes. It's an early summer's day, but one of those wet ones where the wetness translates into a bone-going cold.

I climb onto the frame, pass Fatin my hemp sack of timber wedges, sit on a horizontal bar and place a wedge underneath a moss-patched stone. I push the wedge in until it does not move, so too the next and the next and the next and the next, until I've built up around this stone a sort of cupped flower of wedges. Anna then points out to me a crack in the lime cement and we agree to extend the steel support.

'We may as well patch these joints up today!' I say.

In a stiffening breeze, Anna and I arrive at the other side of the castle, stepping up to a wall edging a steep fall of land. There are persons straggled along it, all tipping and tapping rhythmically while pushing a lime cement into the cavities, shoring this boundary up. Some at the other end are tying down over the work an unruly sheet of shining tarpaulin.

Anna approaches an elderly woman sitting on a stool, who smiles then passes Anna a large bucket filled with this cement. Way above them, a fledgling falcon lifts and descends cumbersomely onto grasses shuddering in the breeze at the top of what's left of a towering finger of stone.

'Grab some trowels there, buck,' Anna says to me as she passes.

I first met Anna when I was in Utrecht and beginning my training in restorative sculpture. She was visiting her girl-friend, one of the other apprentices, a local woman called Dani. Anna was studying in Ireland to be a nurse, but, with each visit to Dani, she took more interest in our work, until she decided to enrol and take up a three-year appren-ticeship, like the one I was a year into. But, where I veered into restorative sculpture, she moved towards the study of ancient structures. Soon after Anna moved over, she and Dani parted ways. I thought Anna would fold and return home, but instead she stayed, good-humouredly learning her trade and improving her Dutch until it was far more sophis-ticated than mine. She worked the same hours as me and, because our workshops neighboured each other, we'd often lunch together and every evening we'd while away the time over cups of cider and the odd cigarette, sharing what we'd learned that day. She'd tease me often, saying that my inter-est in stone sculpture was one merely so as I could attempt to understand the origins of a given stone, hoping to divine what the geological forces might have been that brought this stone into being. I remember laughing this off until I inno-cently told her one day that my father was once a quarryman, and to this she cackled: 'You see! You see!'

She's a talented stonecutter, and trained for years, after Utrecht, at the Stonemasons' Guild of Saint Stephen, in England, becoming an expert in forgotten forms of build-ing, but now she, like me, works more in overseeing projects. Today, though, as we work together with the wedges and this lime cement and trowels, it is as if it's suddenly over

two decades ago and we are back in our twenties again, close
to each other in a cold and noisy string of workshops on the
outskirts of Utrecht.

We have returned to our scaffold and, as Anna and I work in the breeze, she tells me that one half of her restoration is to be shored up and ready for tours by the end of the following year.

She pushes with her nail-bitten fingers a slug of lime cement into a crevasse between two stones. Then, pointing to an inner chamber, its floor flags edged with yellow and white flowers, she says, 'See down there, John? That was once used by the locals here as a handball court, and over there, behind that wall –' and she twists into the wind, pushing her hard hat back off her brow – 'that's apparently where teenagers would go to sing and drink, and many the first snog and feel was copped in there. That's heritage, as well you know,' she says, in her flat south-midlands accent, as she turns back to me, her broad face framed by the ruins behind and the gently rising pasture tumbling away to the right and towards a bend in the river, as it eases off to sea.

She rubs her nose with the back of her wrist and sniffs contentedly.

'And from whom did you hear all this?' I ask.

'Oh, a local one was telling me,' she says. 'I met her at the bingo here, one Thursday.'

I look to Anna, smiling. I lay with the side of my trowel a sliver of cement into a crevasse and push it in with my fingers.

'And does this local lady still go to the bingo on Thursdays?' I ask, tapping the stone with the handle of my trowel.

'She might.'

And there is a pause, and I stop tapping the stone. The wind picks up, and I realise that Anna is now laughing

69

quietly to herself and shaking her head, as if she is thinking of something that she can't or will never quite believe.

'Do you like her?' I say.

Anna's smile broadens and she looks up, her eyes suddenly watering, and says, 'Yeah, she's lovely.'

I arrived back from Anna's restoration late. I was jet-lag tired, so I put myself to bed, and yet, now, struggling to sleep, I decide to reach for my Nokia and send a daring message to Bernadette.

I was wondering if you might like to see if we can find this Schmid?

I put the phone down and wait for it to bleep.

As I lie there, I see *Kritios Boy*'s hips shaking, and a crack forming along his pelvis.

It is as if he is about to step out of himself and begin his fall to the ground.

6

THE QUIET AND UNREPEATABLE
CLOSENESS OF IT

The land outside is dry and the giant fields are shining and flat.

It all passes, at times, with an unearthly smoothness.

Then the carriage bumps and wobbles, lifting me away from this landscape and back into myself.

Opposite slumps a bespectacled old man. One of the lenses in his round steel-rimmed glasses is cracked, while the other shines white, and when it is not shining it hosts a circular reflection of the Polish countryside passing outside, with tiny objects sliding in and out of frame.

Bernadette is in my room, pulling me from my bed. She tells me she's received a message overnight from Schmid's studio in the Muranov part of town, not far from the so-called Palace of Science and Culture.

I put on my trousers and shoes, as Bernadette leads me to her bedroom, where she shows me a map of Warsaw onto which she has drawn a red arrow and circle.

'Here! His workshop!' she says, pointing to the centre of this circle.

I look at her as she puts away this map and folds over a navy woollen jumper on her lap, and it occurs to me that I would like to say to her: *I admire you, Bernadette!*

She peers up at me.

Then, sitting on the side of her bed, she reaches out and takes my left hand in her fingers, holds it there a while and looks at me.

I smile back, but, unprepared for this, I return my hand to my side.

Mr Schmid, a small, balding man in his late sixties, meets us at the entrance to his studio – a large industrial unit, nestled in the corner of a courtyard at the base of the city's old Palace of Science and Culture. As we pass from his foyer – dotted with glass-encased figurative models and maquettes – and into the noisy workshop, fragments of this Gothic-Soviet edifice, framed by tall windows, loom beyond.

'My father was one of thousands who migrated here to build that thing,' he calls back to us in his high-pitched voice, his arm directed towards the window. 'He became lead ceramicist by the end!'

To one side, as Schmid gestures us towards his office, three technicians guide a huge bronze bird into the air. It sways from straps groaning up to the arm of a stout yellow crane. They then lower this soaring bird into a timber pallet box.

'The congress hall inside the palace is really something!' continues Schmid, over his shoulder, as a young woman to our left hammers, in horrible clangs, sparks flying, at a right angle of steel. 'You should visit!'

Mr Schmid opens out a pink folder onto the table and he points to the faded photos and documents within, while describing to us how he received the commission and about the other artists who were then involved. He pulls back a photograph – a close-up of him as a young man, with a full head of dark hair, he speaking with an older man wearing large black-framed glasses. Both are inspecting where Achim's hand tugs at his collar. Sliding out from underneath, another photo shows the whole team on the shop floor, with *1985* written in white at the bottom edge. Schmid names the people, all brandishing welders' masks: 'Hans, Julia, Sergey, Woichech and –' as he comes to the last person in this row of tradespeople, a handsome young woman with bobbed black hair, his finger wavers and his voice cracks almost imperceptibly around her name – 'Magda.'

He looks to us plaintively, helplessly, one of his unruly eyebrows raised, as if he is now stuck and needs us to unstick him and set whatever mechanism is within him back to life.

'May we see the other photo again?' I say.

He slides the photograph across the table.

It's curled and frayed around the edges, and in it I see those two men, their heads dwarfed by Achim's impassive and enormous head, his gazing eyes, and around Achim's neck loops a ratchet strap, tied in a noose, and below and to the right gapes in his chest a hole.

I put my finger to it.

'The joint, yes, yes,' he says, 'where Bettina's back meets Achim's chest.'

Bernadette leans forward, her eyes roaming around this image. I realise this hole is the shape of Achim's waiting, and then the two parts of this troubling sculpture finally slot together in my mind.

Schmid, chuckling gently, shows us another black-and-white photograph, near to the end of the folder, depicting a detail of Bettina's right hand.

'You see ... the fingers and thumb are so,' he says, 'to suggest she is holding a book. This was Magda's thought, that Bettina would be looking up from this as if she had just heard a disturbance in the distance.'

Bernadette, standing beside me in this busy evening bar, looks out over the crowd, who are all much younger than us.

A half dozen or so newcomers enter the front door, greeting other friends as they all slide into the red-lit booths either side of a wall of reflective glass, over which thumps what sounds to me like Polish dance music.

I look to Bernadette a moment, as the music lifts; then, as she turns, I look away.

During our visit this afternoon to the Palace of Science and Culture, we took an elevator to the viewing platform way up on the thirtieth floor. It was blowy and the sky was clearing after a strangely localised shower of rain had fallen in curtains around the high-rises in the middle of the city.

As we were standing in the cool breeze on the platform, both of us looking at the tiny herds of tourists migrating around the red-roofed old town in the distance, Bernadette said, with no heat, that this would be the last place she would ever come to meet me.

I look at Bernadette once more. She's now eased a swathe of hair from her neck. The music in the bar has shifted to something less frenetic and I reckon that, if she were with another person now, they would probably ask her to dance.

My parents met at a dance in a small civic hall two towns west of my home town. Once they had danced together, 'That was it,' my mother often exclaimed. 'That's it – Tom Molloy's the one for me!'

I can feel Bernadette step closer, then drift for a moment away. She is looking out over the crowd again, as if in search of someone she might know.

Bernadette, sipping the last of her orange-coloured cocktail, stands with her back to the bar, still gazing at the crowd.

I turn to her as she puts her glass onto the tabletop, and she silently smiles.

I lean towards her as if to say something into her ear.

As I do so, I can feel the warmth from her cheek meeting the side of my face.

I can smell the musky scent of the soap in her hair, too.

I hesitate, as my heart begins to slow, and I wonder if it might be best simply to make some inane comment half-called into her ear and then step away as if nothing had ever happened.

But I am sure I can feel her now waiting too, and I wonder if her heart is also slowing.

I reckon, if I could see us both in this busy and bright bar, my cheek almost touching hers, I might then see, from her blue eyes, that she looks at least expectant. The warmth radiating from her cheek, I realise, is exceptional.

There's a moment when my lips touch her cheek and I feel her slowly turn her cheek closer to me, and her lips then gently meeting my cheek too, and this sends static shooting down my neck, where it spirals then dissipates at the base of my spine.

I kiss her cheek again – it like the surface of a passing comet – until I feel her shoulder lift and her breath or something in her become halted. I can feel the palm of her hand on the back of my head as she pulls me closer to this small space we've carved out between her cheek, my lips, my eye, my eyelid, her ear, her neck.

She leans back from me a little, looks at me for some moments, and then she places the palm of her hand onto my cheek, and as the bar lights buzz and the neon flickers and the music gently thuds, she looks right into me, her lower lip seeming to tremble in this light.

To all of this I shake, then nod my head.

Her eyes rove over and back across my face, and with this her features change. It is as if she is making some giant calculation.

She drops her hand from my cheek, takes my hand, and we leave the bar and walk.

We arrive at the apartment and she undresses without saying a word. Then she leads me to my bed, where she begins to undress me too. I harden as she kisses me again, and I kiss her back.

Bernadette is now asleep on her side. I lie on my side too, wide awake, looking at the scattering of freckles on her back, her slim shoulders.

I turn onto my back, my cock now limp, and look at the ceiling.

I think about that small, complicated space we carved out in that bar, between her cheek, my lips, my eye socket, her ear, her neck, and I realise that I will never forget, not its shape, but the quiet and unrepeatable closeness of it.

Bernadette is beside me, but still turned away. I can tell that she is not sleeping.

And into this tense silence she seems to ask: *Are you satisfied?*

'No,' I whisper.

She turns and moves towards me as my eyes begin to weaken and close. I feel the warmth of her body settle onto my left flank, and the weight of her head on my arm as she takes my hand too, and I drift back into a deep sleep.

I wake to the dawn light turning the curtains into a wavy plane of glowing blue.

We are apart, again.

I place my hand onto her shoulder and Bernadette turns to me.

Without saying a word, she takes my head in her hands and draws my mouth to hers. We kiss, but this time far more so than before. Then she pulls me to her, then pushes me back.

She smiles and I smile too. She lifts some strands of her hair from across her face. She looks at me again, still in silence, her blue eyes taking me in, her lips as if about to say something.

Then, she shifts onto her back and places her right leg across her left. I see a tattoo of a crucifix on the rear of her knee and a small explosion of crimson veins on her thigh. She pulls my torso once more to hers and reaches down and guides my hardening cock into her. She asks me to touch her breasts. I can feel her hips rock gently for a time, slowly and then more quickly in enlarging and then deepening circles. Then, in the smallest and most gorgeous of pulsations, I begin to come.

Opening my eyes, I see her bring her hand down, and she begins to rub herself for a time, until this quiet rubbing and her breathing deepens. Then her head slowly falls back and her jaw juts, her lips forming a rictus 'o'. She turns her face once more to me as her eyes roll into apple white, and I realise, as our bodies tauten then harden against each other, that she, at this fascinating new distance to me, is about to alter.

7

OVER LAND AND ON TO BOLOGNA

Anna climbs down from a tower of scaffold circling the old castle rampart. More scaffolding rattles on the other side of the wall – its spikes appearing above the stone.

The breeze picks up as Anna walks me around the castle to another wing I'd assumed would be cordoned off and left as 'unsafe ground', but instead there stands a large frame of steel retaining like a giant mandible the most fragile of stone archways.

We inspect where the steel-and-timber meets the stone.

Satisfied with this, she leads me back past stacks of planks, toppled stone, barrels, quaking mounds of tarpaulin, to where she holds open a metal gate leading towards a passage.

We climb a stone spiral so tight that even Anna, who is not a tall woman, has to hunch her broad shoulders as we go. We reach three shallow steps widening onto a floor of scaffold, over which we walk, in clangs, until we arrive at a propped-stone chimney flue, to the right of which a tall window arcs, restored and clear, offering views out over the river and the rolling fields to the southern edge of the town.

'We'll rebuild this whole Hellfire Club too,' she says, arms wide. Then, lifting her hat from her head: 'It will keep me here a while!'

I look out the windows at a murmuration of birds as it dives behind a hill.

'You'll see more of your Patricia,' I say, to which she nods, her pursed lips relenting to a smile.

We look out the windows for a while.

More birds fly by, geese in a 'V', reflected in a calm part of the river, and away.

Then, I tell her about Bernadette. I tell her that I'm going to visit her in Bologna for a fortnight, to see how it might all go.

'You kept that one quiet, buck!' she says.

I smile and kick the ground. 'There was nothing really to say,' I reply.

She shifts her weight and I can feel her study me.

I peer over, probably with a pleading look on my face.

She leans to me and takes my hand, and she tells me not to worry.

'You know it's all quite easy, John, until it isn't,' she says.

Then we descend from the ruin and she walks me to my van to see me off, but before I can get in she grabs me and gives me a long hug.

Through the door at the far end of the light-filled train carriage appears a curly-haired commuter of middle age. He
takes a seat across from a large young man, reading a book. I
look past them at the mountains gathering up into view and
realise how, the last time I was on this train, with the snow
covering up the features of the alpine land, the countryside
had begun to look like a sculpture. Now, though, with the
sun breaking through the windows, and with the slopes and
dips outside all full of life and teeming with trees of countless hues and forms, it is as if the landscape has bred itself
into an altogether different world.

I sit up as the train slows to a halt on a bend in what
seems the middle of nowhere, and I take out a postcard I
purchased yesterday in a shop in the park containing Achim
and Bettina. The postcard features a photograph, from the
early nineties, of this sculpture draped in a thick blanket of
snow. I write onto it a note to Anna, telling her I'm on a train
now and am mere hours from Bologna and Bernadette. Then
I draw a tiny mountaintop underneath where I've written my
name. I return the card to my bag and pull out a photograph
Bernadette sent me a few days ago. It was posted to her by
Mr Schmid; it is a copy of the one showing Achim's head in a
noose, with that cavity of steel at his breast. I decided yesterday afternoon, armed with this photograph, to visit the thing
again, and as I circled the object, all I could remember of
Schmid was his finger shaking with emotion as it pointed out
to us his fellow sculptor Magda. Then, I sat down on a bench
and opened out the photograph showing this young Schmid
inspecting a flaw in Achim's shoulder, and I realised that this

object, though a work made in devotion to this Romantic-era couple, was for Schmid, it seemed to me, a careful expression of his shyness.

Looking at the photograph now on this light-filled train, I think that, while Schmid was making this object, he was trying to tell Magda that he admired her, and that this sculpture is still stating his admiration, but in a way that keeps this statement mountain-ranges out of Magda's earshot, should Magda be able to hear or ever be amenable to hearing it. As the train eases forward again, I consider Schmid's last comment to Bernadette and me, and it begins to make more sense: he told us that he never visited this sculpture in its place. I remember thinking this strange, but now I find his decision a good show of sure-footedness – albeit sure-footedness in an isolated arena – and it occurs to me that he knew the closer he got to the end of the project, the closer he also was to completing his association with this team of collaborators, Magda being chief among them. So, with the installation of this object in the middle of this city, he had successfully completed his complicated act of saying nothing, and he knew there was no need to witness that.

I place the postcard back into my rucksack and take instead this small sandstone caryatid. I decided to bring it with me as a gift for Bernadette. I felt that I'd completed it last week, but looking at it in the sun now, and seeing the shadows falling across her arms and hands, I realise that I'd like to return with a very small rasp and refine the junction between the top of her head and the beginning of the entablature above. I know that this sort of refinement could go on forever, each chisel removing the marks of the previous in ever decreasing perfections, so I wrap the sculpture back up in a shirt and put it away. Last week, before I finished up the sculpture, I read off one of those photocopied sheets of encyclopaedia that the Pentelic marble used in the original statue in the Acropolis was mined from Mount Pentelus of Attica, and this metamorphic stone is of such a yellow hue as to shine gently and translucently in the late evening sun. Perhaps some day I will copy this small sandstone work onto a small piece of Pentelic marble retrieved from Mount Pentelus in Attica …

A plump man appears beside me with a circular tray in his hand, asking if I'd like something from the restaurant.

I ask for a *Weissbier*.

Then, from the end of the carriage, a thin woman in her late fifties enters. She wears hiking gear of light pastel colours. Her blonde-grey hair stands up in wavering lines around her pink headband. As she approaches, broken shafts of light sweeping across her, I see that her small blue eyes, behind rimless glasses, look exhausted. I imagine her earlier in the day, setting out on a trail up a hill covered in swaying trees. She smiles, then she sits a few seats up from me, removes her boots and socks, and stretches out her feet. Her toes are misshapen – like a sandstone peninsula descending into an expanse of ocean.

I turn to the mountainous landscape outside.

The waiter places a golden column of beer on the table in front of me.

Sitting forward, I take a sip from the froth as we swing past a church spire in a valley far below. Then, up slides a mountain peak towards which we speed. The land undulates until we come upon an inclined flank of yellowing acreage where a dozen men work on a road, eight of them shovelling out bitumen before a red roller issuing strings of smoke into the starkly blue sky.

Then the carriage falls into darkness.

We re-emerge once more into daylight, and pass a row of brick houses with protruding front-facing gables topped with the shallowest of shingle roofs. Three pylons rear up in a line behind, slipping in, then out of coalescence. In the foreground, a hotel whooshes past, three gold stars down its side, like those on the lapel of a soldier's uniform, the soldier marching – full of fortitude – across a smoke-edged field towards a setting sun. Canting lines of shivering silver saplings swerve down and out across a giant stretch of wind-whipped green, leading to a road and, beyond it, a lemoning embankment that unfurls into the foothills of a mountain. The road zigzags up the mountain, disappearing and reappearing as it leads to a white church surrounded by bright red houses of single and two storeys. An old castle overhangs it all – its toothsome facade gazing brazenly back across the valley at me. To the south, up surges a leaning plane of granite, shot through with huge arteries of sandstone. Someone coughs loudly behind. A train rushes past, shuddering my carriage and blocking the view, reducing my eyes to mere objects tracing sine waves of red and white until this speeding train disappears, with a shriek, and our carriage eases out of its shudder and I can see in the distance the inward folds of a falling plain into which runs a busy motorway, its fumes throwing the midday light between here and there into a romantic haze. The train slows as we ascend, and then turns up out of this valley till we fall parallel with a broad bend in the motorway beneath, us now surging past lorries and cars and trucks, until suddenly a lengthy row of trees zips up the view.

I sit back a while and close my eyes and feel the light outside pass and quake and pass.

We slow, stop, speed up and slow again.

I open my eyes and glance across the aisle. The hiker is fast asleep, her feet spread out before her, her fingers twitching gently on her lap, her mouth open as if in prayer. I take the world as being in order and I close my eyes for a while, to see if I might gain a view onto the dreamscape of this sleeping hiker.

Nothing.

I open my eyes, and to my left I spy along the side of the mountain three large birds descending onto mile-long swoops of electrical cables – one, two, three, four, five – connecting this valley to the next and to the next. More rows of these curious saplings appear down to the fore, while in the distance climb houses and shining green trees and slip roads, and in the growing heat of the carriage I wonder how the air up there must feel and if this is the kind of air of which the sleeping hiker is dreaming.

I sit back and sip my beer as another train thumps past; it is laden with gleaming automobiles, all heading north.

A canal swings parallel for a while, then disappears some-where underneath, and as we swerve left I can see a town with single-storey houses murmuring up to a tower made of reddening brick. Beyond this, the land lifts again, with the sun rippling across the rock face, all of its giant rocks shining like tombstones. An onion dome pops up deep in the valley, and a bell tower with white clock faces on its facades.

A building site passes. It is derelict and the one tower crane within has collapsed from a 'T' into an 'R'.

Behind this, upon a sheltering ridge, stand three pylons of different design, side by side, like haunted pilgrims sur-veying the riches below. An oval-shaped football stadium swims down into view, while around it surges a river of the palest green – the Etsch. Thirty or so figures stand around the centre circle of this pitch, being lectured to by a track-suited figure while a constellation of glowing footballs dot out the field. All of the buildings surrounding are threaded through by this green river that, as it swings frothing and twisting towards the train, turns into the shuttering rush of a passing bridge truss, which collapses from view, then is replaced with splayed concrete legs thrusting up to a roadway snaking across the sky, until all of this is met by the ear-popping darkness of a tunnel.

The tunnel lamps strobe as they pass on and on, in a dotted line of light inclined out into the black. I put my fingers to my nose and blow out, reinflating what has col-lapsed within my ears. I look on at the angled line of white until this progression into the dark is, from nowhere, deci-mated by a trumpet-blast of form and colour, cut through with more concrete pillars, legs, undercarriages, wires, pylons, steeples, shadows and a distant stand of old Roman towers and older castles teetering upon even older outcrops of grey and ancient limestone. The land then falls away and more railway lines appear below. A curve sweeps us past a lumber yard, shining in the heat, the timber in stacks all surrounded by sprinklers issuing arcs of sparkling water upon the boles, suggesting these great masses, for a moment, are mere kindling. The river swerves around and past this lumber yard and, before it meets us again, we enter yet another tunnel of total darkness from which appears, as we emerge back out onto the sunlit land, a peak split by a climbing gorge full of giant boulders leading up to a knuckle covered in the greenest of trees all shivering skyward, over which grows, like an angel in the sky, a churning cloud of sparkling white.

The hiker rouses, smacks her lips and sits up.

I lean forward and take a sip from my flat and warming beer.

Another passenger train thuds by, revealing, on its passing, a gnarled upgrowth of Dolomiten land, pitted with apple-bite indentations on its green and yellowing flanks.

More glinting pylons descend, in increments, from this peak. Cables droop almost to the ground; fields sway with lavender.

A ruin comes and goes.

A white bridge off to the left spans over both arms of the forking river, as one distributary surges down into the distance and away.

Tiny allotments containing lines of tomato plants, walled in a stone boundary covered over in graffiti, run up onto an embankment that peters out behind a cuboid of tinted glass, reflecting all around it. My carriage lifts and swerves above some rooftops that grow into buildings of three and four storeys, all leading into the northern edge of Trento, and we begin once more to slow.

It darkens, and then rain, as we pull away from Trento station, begins to fall. As the town disappears behind us, I spy, out the opposite window and halfway up the lush valley in the distance, a stray cloud. I watch it float in its own weft and warp as it sails across the valley, revealing, on the lustrous incline behind, a row of poplars climbing a hill that leads to a house of two storeys, to the right of which stands a tower, roofless and in the early stages of collapse. The cloud floats into our train carriage and stalls a moment above the dozing hiker's head before it fizzles into a constellation of smaller fizzling fibres, all drifting now in their altering ordinates further and further away from each other. The mountains too begin to collapse around me, into hills, then muffled plains of mostly green and yellow and brown, upon which appears the odd church steeple and tower, bare now on the flat lands, their upward thrusts unframed and desolate.

It is exceptionally hot, and even though it is late evening, it still seems exceptionally bright as I step down from the train to disembark into Bologna Centrale.

In between the elephant calls of the trains, I can hear the chirruping of cicadas.

I descend into a network of cool tunnels and let the mass of travellers lead me up to the front entrance of the station.

My heart quickens as I walk across the concourse and out into the blinding evening sun.

I push my hair from my forehead as I, somewhat short of breath, look about the broad piazza at the currents of people rushing to buses, jumping into honking cars, or filing around traffic lights.

And then, there, standing across a slip road to the front of the station, is Bernadette.

She wears a navy sleeveless dress and a pair of navy running shoes. Her hair is gathered up in a large bun with a slim stick through it. She is peering the other way, across the piazza, at a commotion involving police and a collection of young women all wearing long patterned dresses and red headscarves. More of these women, some carrying young children, crowd around a ticket machine at a bus stop, which is already crowded with large pale tourists awaiting an airport bus.

As Bernadette turns towards me, I see a girl is with her. Bernadette waves and is smiling widely, but my attention is drawn to this dark-haired girl, Philomena, who is not smiling at all. I would say that she is frowning.

Though Bernadette has shown me photographs of Philomena before, I am not prepared for the similarity between their faces, both together here, in actuality.

A red bus trundles by, blasting dust and exhaust into the air.

I look across the slim slip road once more to Philomena's frowning face and then to Bernadette's smiling face, and I realise that, despite the difference in their age, there is a logic to their facial resemblances, but that this logic is itself invisible or simply elsewhere, or, at the very least – as one of my bags drops from my hands – it is indescribable, and this, for more than just a startling moment, reminds me of my mother and makes me terribly unnerved.

Then, unsure of what else to do, I pick up my bag and go to Bernadette.

She greets me with a tight hug, a kiss on the cheek, and for a moment she squeezes my arm, which I realise is shaking. She looks me in the eyes, the evening sun shifting across her irises, and she silently smiles even more so than before. Then she turns to Philomena, now stepping out from behind her, and Philomena offers me her small hand, which I take, and I shake it gently and say, 'You must be Philomena, so. I'm John. It's lovely to meet you.'

She screws her face up and looks to her mother, as if to say, *What did this strange man just utter?*

Then she looks at me and says in stilted, rehearsed English, 'Welcome to Bologna, John.'

In the car back across the sweltering old city, Philomena and Bernadette speak to each other in Italian. I can tell that Philomena is being difficult, knowing her mother will be slow to anger in front of this man in the passenger seat of their car. The narrow and busy streets lined with red-brick buildings festooned with crimson canopies glide by.

As we leave the city walls and turn onto a carriageway heading east, Philomena asks Bernadette a question with the word 'Papa' at the end of it, and to this Bernadette peers into the rear-view mirror, unimpressed, then merely raises her eyebrows and silently glowers. I can hear Philomena laugh and then slump back onto the rear seat in a sort of bored huff, which lasts mere minutes, before she leans forward once more and asks me how long I will be in Bologna.

'Just two weeks,' I say, as we turn off this carriageway and into an underground car park beneath a medium-rise tower of shining white apartments.

'And do you like to eat fish?' asks Philomena.

'Oh, *sì*!' I say.

And to this she smiles goofily, and, as the car comes to a halt beside a glossy bush of rosemary protruding heroically from a concrete pot, she jumps out, swinging her red jumper over her head.

Bernadette then turns to me and kisses me on the mouth.

I wake in the night to a strange creak from the floor above. It takes a while for me to realise where I am.

In the sultry darkness, I remember a strange moment from this evening while I was unpacking my toiletries in Bernadette's en suite and I did not know where to put them in among her things. She seemed to have cleared a section to the right of her toothbrush, floss and face cream, so I merely placed my toiletry bag in there, leaving my toothbrush within. It seemed too bold to take my toothbrush out and just place it there on the shelf. I wondered at the time what other small habits of living I was intruding into, and part of me, at the thought of the intimate complexity of such things, wanted to leave there and then, but instead I rejoined the two of them at the kitchen table, where Philomena was doing some colouring on a newspaper and Bernadette was opening a bottle of white wine. I lifted from my rucksack and gifted Bernadette the small sandstone caryatid I'd made, and as she took it in her hands I could see her eyes at once open in surprise and begin to water, and it occurred to me that she might not have been gifted anything for quite a while. Philomena then came over and looked the object up and down as it was being rotated in her mother's hands, and then she, smiling shyly, uttered an elongated, '*Che bellllla.*'

I roll over to my left and take Bernadette into my arms. She sleepily rubs my hand, and I fall once more to sleep.

Next day, after a lunch of tomato pasta and a dessert of home-made tiramisu, we take a drive out of the tacky humidity of the city to a gorge. Philomena and Bernadette direct me from the all-but-empty car park down through a series of narrowing paths. The sun is high in the sky, and the rough sandstone walls of the small canyon enlarge and deepen as we go. Cicadas chirrup in great waves around us and tiny lizards zigzag about in the sand and loam at our feet.

Soon, we arrive at a circular, freshwater pool. On the northern side shivers a stand of fig trees among a rising of crags.

Philomena and Bernadette step into the shade, open their towels onto the ground and remove their clothes down to their swimming costumes underneath. Then Philomena takes a running jump and a splash. Bernadette steps down carefully into the black water, her arms spread out either side, as if she were on a tightrope, her lips pouting with the pleasant-seeming chill. She descends right up to her neck and makes an easy breaststroke loop around where Philomena's head and torso suddenly re-emerge. I put my hand to my brow, to shield my eyes against the sun and the sparkles from the water far below. I can feel the heat upon the top of my head as I look on at these two figures treading water.

'Are you coming in?' calls Philomena, bobbing about.

'Maybe he doesn't swim,' says Bernadette. 'It's OK, John, if you don't!' she adds, smiling, between sharp intakes of breath.

I can see the frizzy tips of Bernadette's hair droop into the water and fan out like a vast halo around her shoulders. I falter for many moments, imagining the strange figure they are now looking back up at on the shore: a slim and dark-haired man with his hand above his brow, the sky and rocks edging out his body, shining blue and white behind.

Then, as if stepping out of something that has encapsulated me for some time, I lean forward and pull off my dusty boots, remove my shirt, my socks, my trousers, and, with the sunlight sharp upon my exposed body, I step down shakily towards the cool and oily water.

PART II

A LETTER FROM HOME

It is the morning after my fifty-sixth birthday.

I wake, dry-mouthed, in bed beside Bernadette. It's warm, or at least I can feel that mid-summer heat enlarging outside – a heat in which, after ten years here, I am still not wholly comfortable. Bernadette is turned towards me, breathing deeply, her eye mask slipped up onto her forehead. I replace it over her eyes. Then, I listen to the cicadas outside and I realise today will be another one filled with their rapturous bassy cacophony, opening and closing in swirls around the city.

I rise and go to the kitchen to fill two glasses with water.

We spent my birthday at a beach in Rimini, surrounded by golden bathers standing knee-deep in the Adriatic, splashing water over themselves before leaving the lilting sea and taking to their sunloungers. We did this for almost the entire day – sun, salt water, shade, drinks, reading. In the evening, after a busy train ride back, Bernadette and I had a meal in our regular bistro in the centre of town – a simple bowl of sage ravioli – after which we watched an old Italian cowboy film in the outdoor cinema set up for this week every year in

Piazza Maggiore. Then, passing the shadow of the statue of Hermes cast high upon the walls of the Palazzo Comunale, we wandered home, stopping in the evening heat for a beer at a small terraced bar.

White morning light pours in through the kitchen's balcony door and falls across the small jungle of climbing plants and ferns that Bernadette and I have arranged here for the summer.

It's a Monday, but I decided months ago to take this week off work and to extend my birthday into a home holiday. I can sense the morning traffic outside zooming up and easing down the hill.

There's a note scribbled on a piece of yellow paper, folded into an apex on the table. It's from Philomena: *See you at the Elite for lunch break, John!* To the right lies splayed the early-morning post of three bills and a letter, behind which teeters a stack of Bernadette's English tutorial papers.

I sift through the envelopes as I sip from my water, and note the letter has an Irish postmark. As I open it, out slips a single sheet of lined paper, written upon in handwriting unfamiliar to me. From one of the folds drops a photograph of Anna and her Patricia, sitting on a stone wall, smiling and leaning into each other, the wind playing with their hair. A yellow beach stretches out into a broad arc in the distance behind.

I turn the photograph. *July 2017* is written in the bottom corner.

The letter is from Patricia and she tells me that Anna is dying and is in pain. She tells me that she has contacted everyone who was or is close to Anna, and that, whether they are religious or not, she is asking these friends to pray for Anna's speedy death. She says that Anna requested she do this for her a fortnight ago. Patricia then says that, even though she will miss her *dear Anna* terribly, she herself is praying *daily to God* to hasten Anna's last breath. She asks me sincerely to do the same.

I fold the letter over and look once more at the photograph of them twelve months ago in this coastal setting.

I make a coffee and, as it brews on the stove, I walk out to the broad, plant-lined balcony. The tiles beneath my feet are warm, and dusty with pollen and seeds. Leaning on the ivy-twisted railing of the north-facing parapet, I can see wavering in the heat Bologna's ancient skyline of canting towers, old churches, spires and treetops. Below, Francisco, Bernadette's uncle, opens up in squeaks and shunts his furniture workshop. Soon he'll have an unlit cigar in his mouth, and by lunch he will light it and let it burn and go out and burn and go out for the rest of the day, drawing on the smoke as he happily moves around, cutting, tacking, hammering, glueing, singing.

I try to think of the last time I saw Anna.

Then, with the coffee beginning to whistle, I return indoors and pour myself a cup, and make off towards the bedroom with a glass of water for Bernadette.

A rectangle of bright morning light breaks across Bernadette's chin and cheek. Her mask has fallen from her eyes once more, but she is deep in sleep. I place the glass of water by her bedside, kiss her on the forehead, then I go to the window and release the *tenda* another inch or two until the light across her face disappears and the whole room falls into a pensive reddened dark.

I pull on some clothes and return to the kitchen, take another mouthful of coffee and put the letter into my pocket. I turn Philomena's message over and write on the other side a note to Bernadette saying that I've gone out for a walk.

From the hook beside the front door, I lift my keys and step out onto the steep slope of Via dell'Osservanza and let gravity take me towards the junction where I usually stop for a morning coffee and sweet bread, but instead today I turn into the sun, cross the broad and busy Viala Aldini and make my way up into the lines, curves, cobbles and brick walls of the old town.

2

THE RIPENING THOUGHTS
OF ANOTHER MAN

On the front terrace of Caffe D'Azeglio, after ordering a water and a black coffee, I take out the letter and read it through, this time more carefully. I notice, at the end, after Patricia has signed her name, a mobile-phone number.

Into my phone, I type: *Patricia? It's John Molloy.*

I sit back as a skinny youth puts my coffee and water down onto the table.

The phone dings with a text saying: *John. I hope you are well. It's Patricia. You must have received my letter. I'm so sorry. Anna's weak now, but still … she gets these spasms of pain that the doctors can't make sense of.*

I text back: *Will it be long?*

I hope not, she replies.

Then, some moments later, this comes through: :-(

I look for a while at these three tiny glyphs and consider the nature of what they are being asked to portray. I text back saying how sorry I am to hear all of this and that I would like her to tell Anna that I will miss her. I say I had no idea she was so sick. I realise as I type the words that they impotently precede a scale of sadness – a vacating sadness – that I've not felt since my mother went.

The owner of the café brings out two coffees for a young couple smoking at the far side of the entrance.

My phone dings again.

She can't hear or really see anymore, comes the reply.

I can feel my eyes water. I imagine pain must come horribly in the dark.

A small man with a broad mop cleans the terrazzo to the front of the café. I've had many coffees and waters outside of this café on my way to work at a family-run joiners across town, and yet I have never really looked at this sheet of dazzling terrazzo on the ground. I stare at the dark constellations of tiny stones set into the slab. I stare with the understanding that I would rather stare at this than try to compute what is happening to Anna and what I should do, if anything. I wonder if doing nothing at all will help her best – might my doing nothing but just sitting here contribute to a more speedy death? Surely it wouldn't prolong it.

The owner of the café steps back out, now smoking stylishly as he stalks the extents of his terrain. Inside, over shelves on the right-hand wall, hangs a framed painting of this tall and dark-haired man with his arm around the shoulders of a man several years his senior, and I imagine this older man is his father and I imagine the day this father left this café to his son was a happy one. He finishes his cigarette, blowing a jet of smoke from the side of his lips up into the air while scowling at a van poorly parked across the road. The driver of this van appears from the clapping front door of the *studio legale* opposite, and the café owner lifts his arms while calling over the road at this driver, who dismisses him with a flick of his wrist, as if the café owner were little more than a troublesome housefly. The owner turns to me and shrugs as if to say, *Can you believe this man?* I shake my head and realise this café owner has probably had a life so easy as to be always on the cusp of boredom. The van drives off north.

My workplace is just past the northern edge of the old city wall, in an industrial unit on the broad workaday Via Cassarini, where I've been employed for the last eight years or so as a designer and fitter of eco- and ergo-friendly timber playgrounds. During my last few years in the US, I worked with an alcoholic carpenter in Philadelphia. He was from the south-east of Ireland, and, from seven in the morning to noon each day, he'd wander black-eyed around the building we were working on, groaning and pretending to do some work. Then, after usually an enormous lunch of the greasiest of fast food, he'd work feverishly until seven or eight in the evening, carrying out with extraordinary efficiency the work of three normal carpenters. When he'd drop me back to my lodgings in his van, he'd invite me out for a drink, but I rarely went. I lived the solitary, disciplined life of the emigrant saving money. I was essentially this man's apprentice and from him I learned more than just the basics in timber jointing and construction – by the time I left him, I was more or less adept. It was these skills I brought with me to the playground company, the owner of which was a close friend of Francisco, Bernadette's uncle. After a year or so, I began to suggest they look at – as ideas for playgrounds – zoos and building sites, and sort of meld these environments together into one. These new sets of designs seemed to secure the company the contracts on most of the new children's public playgrounds in the Bologna suburbs – and secured me my work with them too.

Any day I walk alone to work, this is the route I take. But, whenever I walk with Philomena, we take a route that leads us first to the mobile-phone shop she works in on the stately, if chaotic, Via dell'Indipendenza. She'll be in there now, showing phone accessories to customers. She's saving to leave Bologna soon with her boyfriend, Henry, an American student she met while studying undergraduate history in the university here. He seems like a nice boy and is handsome, but he has an amount of confidence I find unnerving. He seems to live in a world free of doubt. Bernadette says she's excited for Philomena planning her adventures away from us here, but I know, the morning that Philomena eventually leaves, Bernadette will be terribly upset.

I drop two euro on the table and make my way down the street and past the broad Hydra Building with its sumptuous front garden, in the middle of which stands a silent, dry fountain.

As I go, it occurs to me that I've not once prayed or even thought of praying since my mother went, and even then I could only bear such a thing for the thought of her safe passage. I feared then, and I realise that I still fear now, the act of praying, because of the fissures it brought to my mother's mind and the destruction it wreaked on her life. I am not sure if it is that I am not able to pray for Anna, or that I am afraid to pray, in case, by doing such a thing, I too will bring destruction to those around me.

I look up and spy in the distance Bernadette's church, the great Corpus Domini, as it looms into view.

The sun is spearing through the church's upper dome while collapsing in bent oblongs across the floor and walls below.

The glinting interior – reaching out in front and way above me – is wholly empty of people. As I step inside, I realise I've not been in this place for some time, perhaps since I first arrived here in Bologna and Bernadette and I attended a rather joyful christening. Bernadette has mentioned often to me how much she likes this building's humble exterior, with the great riches and space inside. She has said it is a place that helps order her thoughts.

Bernadette's faith is something that has grown in her over the years, and yet it still seems to be a strictly private thing. I remember asking her one day a few years back, when I walked into the sitting room in our old apartment on the eastern edge of town, why she was kneeling at the window and praying. She looked at me for some moments, gauging whether she should answer and, if she should, what kind of answer she might give. She told me that she would need some belief or at least the habit of faith to prepare her, she gesturing towards the sun outside, for the inevitable encroaching dark. Then, a few days later, at breakfast, unbidden, she brought it up again, as if to clarify, and she told me that she had come to prefer the science of religion because it had a procedure that was not of progress or order, but one surrounded by chaos, 'like a drop of mercury falling through a storm,' she said, before she stood to refill her cup.

Across the nave, an elderly man steps out from behind the huge creaking door of a side chapel. Giant statues of

Moses and Aaron brandishing tablets cant from the shadows above him, posturing high up in recesses, one either side of a dramatic tableau of sculpture, relief and candles, all surrounding a painting of God and Christ flanking the planet Earth, with a crucifix at the North Pole, over which floats the image of a glowing dove. This tableau produces such an odd perspective on the door that it seems the elderly man, who now looks tiny, has just entered the dimensions of an obscure Mannerist painting. He sees me peering at him, then he nods and disappears.

Hearing a shuffle from behind, I look over my shoulder at a dark-haired man of middle age stepping out from a distant confessional box. He dries his eyes, which are averted from the rest of the chamber, as if he cannot bear to look into this arena of supposed blessedness. He crosses himself several times, turns and leaves the church. Some moments later, a plump little priest steps from the swishing curtains of this same confessional. I'd describe his facial expression as troubled. He genuflects, then disappears through a side door, carrying with him, I imagine, the ripening thoughts of this other man.

A bird swings past in the sky outside, its rune form flitting through an upper dome window, leaving streaks of shadow upon the bright bands of marble below. The same shaft of glass-warped light has crept onto a pale knuckle of decoration thrusting out at mid-height on the crossing wall, while way behind this knot of gold and alabaster looms the altar, behind which glints a giant oil painting of Christ outside a temple, healing the eyes of a blind man. I see Anna in a bed, eyes closed and tubes entering and leaving her arms and torso, and I will this body to twitch and for the eyes somehow to open. I look around once more at this religious edifice and realise that not one fragment of it has been left unturned to the glory of God, and I realise too how gross a display it is of excess. It strikes me that, if this is Bernadette's preferred place of worship, then it must say something about her state of worship, too, and I imagine, if I were ever privy to a view of her inner place of prayer, that I would not like what I would see.

I bend my head in a paltry attempt to pray. I whisper some indistinct and mind-blanking sentences towards the ground.

In the dark behind my eyes, I don't sense space so much as the sound of stone, a low rumbling groan, and I know if I continue looking into this darkness that this roll of stone-meeting-stone will grow and become unbearable – or, worse, the light that might emerge from behind these shifting stones would be of a kind I cannot unsee. I feel my chest tighten, so I open my eyes and rise.

As I leave, I come upon a side chapel whose ceiling fresco is so war-damaged that all that's visible is a kneeling figure, head craned skyward, offering their adulation to a sky that no longer exists, while, to the right, alongside the door through which the troubled priest had disappeared not minutes ago, stands another confessional. I step to the sinners' side and peer into the darkness beyond the grille. Then I realise that the grille itself has been worn down into what looks like the outline of a face, and I wonder if the shape of that worn piece of brass came about by the absent-minded fingering of sinner after sinner upon its surface, or if the metal has merely been corroded over the years by the breath and voice of transgression.

3

FAINTING BOY

I make my way past one of the remaining city gates, Porta Saragozza. It is shrouded in scaffold. The dust-dry boulevard beyond continues in perspective lines for miles. Sweat courses down my back, and my chest now feels as if someone has slowly loosened a hot strap from around it.

Cars whir by as I step into the shade of the lectern aisle of Via Saragozza. Most of this portico is leaning to the right, as if the buildings flanking it are sinking and drawing with them this shining walkway of columns and arches. I pass hairdressers, cafés brimming with people, and desolate fruit shops from which, as I walk, cool citric air wafts. The sun disappears then comes to again, drawing dark interlinked arcs along the ground, while far off to the left appear the risings of large houses in a heat haze, surrounded by trees clicking with countless cicadas. More houses climb in wide curves up the hill towards the south, where Bernadette, I imagine, still sleeps or perhaps is reading my note while pottering around fixing a coffee, or opening out her folders of English tutorials, or leaning over our balcony and chatting with her uncle, Francisco, of whom she is very fond. I look at my phone and see it is already almost midday and that the battery is running low.

At a junction empty of traffic, the cicadas' clicking surges into a roar once more. As I cross onto Via Filippo Turati, where a block of white apartments replaces the trees, the cicadas' calling falls away and with it all the noise of the city too.

For a moment more, I stall in the growing heat. Most of the shutters on the buildings around me are closed and the streets are suddenly empty.

Then, I hear a creak from above as a pair of shutters come together and I imagine the person who closed these shutters, now far behind this facade, reclining onto a cool bed, hand to brow and slowing into sleep, their heartbeat receding into the hush of a wave breaking onto a distant shore of shale, shifting and loosening, until their breathing all but disappears.

While I walk along this brightening street, I remember Bernadette once telling me how important this Turati was to her when she was in her twenties and studying the origins of Italian socialism. She told me back then about an Anna Kuliscioff, whom Turati had married. Apparently, it was she who influenced him into this anarchist world where he stayed, opposing, like her, the fascism growing then in the country. Bernadette once took me to Milan to visit a bas relief of this couple on the eaves wall of Kuliscioff's old home in the middle of a large piazza, the name of which I cannot remember. She was working on a project, now abandoned, photographing plaques and memorials to socialism in northern Italy. We spoke for some time about bas reliefs in general, and I remember describing to Bernadette a remarkable bas relief I'd seen once in a museum in Washington, of Cain laying Abel to waste. I claimed at the time that this scene was far more powerful because it was a bas relief, and not the same scene depicted in a free-standing sculpture or in a drawing or painting. I remember claiming, or at least I remember thinking that the content of the image was inextricable from the medium because, in the relief, Cain's dominant figure is sculpted free of the marble slab, and Abel, who is being destroyed, is being pushed back into nothingness by his being forced into the inexpressive flatness of the parent stone from which these figures were divined. I said to Bernadette that this pushing of Abel's shoulders, body and face had produced the strangest sculptural bend across his features, from form to flatness, almost as if Abel, at the moment of his annihilation, was entering a black hole on the edge of the cosmos from where his body would distort and never re-emerge. Bernadette then ran her fingers over Turati's broad face ... All of this happened soon after I arrived here, and it occurs to me that, over the years since, I have not sculpted in stone once and that Bernadette and I have worked less and less, to the point now of nothing, on projects of an artistic kind, as if our enthusiasm for such things that brought us together in the first place has been kicked away and we have forgotten about it all – it is as if we have at once forgotten our old and got lost in our new selves, and the habits we have nurtured and then hardened into together have led us away from what was once singular and forceful in our curiosities. I halt a moment on the bright concrete footpath and wonder if this happy direction we've gone in is a good one, and if it is not the case that Bernadette and I have overwhelmed our most native curiosities with metronomic tides of habit that belong, I reckon now, to a sea of the most meagre dimensions with accretions of shingle as the shore that someday late in life I might turn and point to as having meaning, only to realise that these beaches have been blown away, and that I'm gesturing at nothing at all.

A man in a navy suit ticks towards me, cycling a vintage pushbike. His hair is short and white and fashioned into a 'V' that arrows towards the middle of his brow, which furrows as he passes, eyeing me suspiciously. I look at him as he sails off down the street.

Sweat trickles in more rivulets down my back as I enter a path leading into the old town, whereupon four men appear. One holds a ball of string, one a levelling stick, while two are bent over, engaged, sweating and smoking, in a pathway-length riddle of replacing cobblestones.

I pass, bidding them a tentative hello, to which but one, through an exhalation of smoke, responds with a cursory, '*Ciao ragazzo.*'

Continuing up Via Andrea Costa, I cross the dual carriageway and re-enter the city walls, where I spy a café in the cool shade. A scattering of young men in red-and-purple Bologna FC shirts are loitering and laughing in the breeze as they drink lemonade and smoke slim cigars.

I take a seat under a parasol across from a middle-aged couple who are theatrically discussing a gift for a friend – a vanity case. The woman, in a turquoise singlet, floral pants and white sandals, is playing coquettishly with her greying hair while she laughs wheezily at a joke the man, whom I take to be her husband, has just made. Around her bare right ankle drapes a diamanté bracelet, twinkling in the sun, and I picture this woman as an ancient naked cherub at the foot of a vast holy picture, her torso twisted around a bugle, her ankle sparkling. This is one of the things I've come to like about living here, the way the people dress, with almost always something surprising, even daring in their attire, something to draw the eye towards and wonder about. There is a seeming idleness in these flourishes that has nothing idle or extraneous about it – it is as if they offer a direct line into the nature of the person they adorn. I look up as a young couple pass on the street pulling their roller bags after them in a growing hum, and around whom now veers a moped zooming away with a stack of pizza boxes strapped down onto its rear. The shutters of the *marmista* next door clatter up while I down the glass of water the owner moments before slid onto my table, and I place by way of payment a euro coin under the glass.

The middle-aged couple stand to leave, as do I. They go left, chatting away, but I continue down Via Isaiah and on towards Chiesa San Paolo, now glowing before me in the distance, where one day five years ago, when Anna and Patricia visited to celebrate Anna's retirement and their engagement, we brought them to witness the evening light fall across the holy statues gazing out from the west-facing wall.

I found Anna and Patricia, who stayed a week with us, were almost childishly playful with each other. I'd never wholly seen that side of Anna before – her great playfulness – and within it I could see more clearly her wit and how intelligent and quick her sense of humour was, especially in the way she toyed with phrases while making – at first, to me – almost unnoticeable puns on words.

I remember after we left that church saying to them all that it smelt at times in there, as if someone had broken wind. To which Anna, moments later, said, as droll as ever, 'Sure, maybe you were just sitting in someone else's *pew*, John!

And on these at times subtle and, at more times, plainly rude puns would go, until I at last noticed, whereupon she'd

burst out laughing while nudging me mischievously. I liked
Patricia for revealing this aspect of Anna, this splendid ore.

At the side of an otherwise empty length of portico, an emaciated man with a short dark beard lies, passed out in a recess of blue marble. From his upper arm protrudes a scaffold of steel pins, all piercing his flesh with crusting droplets of blood below, and I recall the steel-pin frame that surrounded my shin all those years ago, fusing it back together, and I remember the dizzy feeling, too, on the first day I put weight back on this bone. For several unnerving weeks, it felt as though my leg was too short.

This man before me is deep in a peaceful-seeming sleep, and emits from his nose a wheeze, which recedes as I walk on, and I see in my mind's eye an altar boy swooning to the ground in a cavernous church in my home town, on an especially sunny Easter Saturday, while countless churchgoers queue to kiss the feet of the statue of Christ. As the figure of this altar boy disappears with a thump groundward, all that replaces him is a puff of sun-holding incense, while from across the nave comes the flutter of vestments as the surrounding altar boys dive to his aid. I wonder if this boy I am seeing is me or some other boy with whom I once worked the altar, or perhaps it is a boy I once saw faint in the middle of a lengthy service, when I was very young and attending an Easter Mass with my mother, me sitting safely beside her in a distant seat, yet filled with the feeling: I'm glad that fainting boy is not me.

4

CHORUSES

At the entrance to Chiesa San Paolo, a frail old lady with white hair and large pink-framed glasses insists to me that the place is closed – that the congregation is away for the whole of July and August.

'*Pausa*,' she says, slicing the air with her hands, her tiny grey eyes adamant behind her glasses.

Backing into the shade of the church spire, I look out over the road at the passing streams of mopeds and pedestrians. I take out my phone and realise that, with the battery so low, if I don't ring Bernadette now, then I won't be able to contact her for the rest of the day, and I am not yet ready to go back to our house. Her phone rings twice. Then, she answers with her lovely rustic, '*Pronto*.'

I ask her how she is, to which she replies, yawning, 'OK. Tired, but OK. Where are you?'

'In town,' I say. 'I went for a walk. To clear my head.'

'OK,' she replies, waiting for me to add to this.

But, for some reason, I do not add to this.

'Are you OK?' she asks.

'Yes,' I say, 'I'm fine. I just need to clear my head.'

'OK,' she says, in what I take to be forced insouciance.

'OK,' I say. 'And thank you for the lovely day yesterday. The beach was wonderful, and the food and the film, too. Nothing could have been better.'

'I loved it too,' she says. 'And are we still to meet for lunch with Philomena?'

'Oh, of course,' I say.

'The usual *osteria* on Urbana?'

'Yes, yes,' I say. '*Perfetto!* And can you tell Philomena to meet us there instead of the Elite?'

And, in the middle of her reply, my phone cuts out.

At Porta Nova, I arrive at a small *farmacia* where, soon after I first came to Bologna, I used to purchase medication for a profound and extended bout of insomnia. The two women who ran the pharmacy – mother and daughter – would look at my eyes, inspecting my enlarging and darkening bags, and tut. I felt guilty at the time, not so much for deciding to stay in Bologna with Bernadette, but more so for simply not returning home. Soon this feeling of guilt passed, and when sleep began coming again and I started to look less spent, these women in this pharmacy, as if intuiting the returning vigour, would spend longer chatting with me, chuckling at my broken Italian, and then wave me off, until I needed to see them less and less, and I now realise I have not seen either of them for some time.

Neither, however, is working today. As the young man behind the counter of polished-wood and glass hands me a bottle of water and two sachets of lemon electrolyte, I ask him if these ladies still work here at all.

'They're on holiday,' he replies, 'for two weeks, in Fano!'

I imagine them both reclining on sunloungers, reading in a blossom of shade some untaxing magazine or book, and every now and then walking down to the water and splashing it upon their flanks and legs, and returning with sand gathering on their feet. I resolve to return here soon and see how their spirits are keeping. Then, I step back outside, pour one of the sachets into my bottle of water and shake it milky. As I tilt my head and pour this liquid down my throat, I spy a multi-coloured statue of Saint Salvadore perched upon a raised plinth protruding from the corner of the building opposite. I follow his gaze to the steps leading up into Chiesa della San Salvadore, its front facade covered over in shining and rustling nets draped around a scaffold, within which men shift hither and thither, their silhouettes leaning into the church face and emitting an arhythmic clanking of metal on stone. Looking on at this work, I picture the three trestle tables in my old apartment back home and it occurs to me that I have not thought about the sculptural or geological properties of stone for an age. I realise that my interest in this has waned over these years here, being surrounded by such plenty, such a daily surfeit of religious stonework, and this abundance has produced a numbness, a blindness which I seem to have gladly embraced.

I leave, then round into a section of broad piazza where the sun has drawn out a chiaroscuro shadow over a scattering of tables full of elderly Bolognese drinking ice-crammed Aperol spritzes and small black coffees.

A skinny and dark-haired man on a bicycle rattles to a halt on the street beside me, dismounts and genuflects in through the open doors of a tall and narrow church. I turn to see what he can see, but the innards are shrouded in a complicated darkness.

Beyond the fine old drapery Danesi, I rejoin lower Via D'Azeglio as a line of men with scaffolding tubes stomps past. A pale young family strings by, all in navy shirts and shorts, white socks and shining shoes. Two whistling men, window cleaners, one short with a ladder, the other tall with a sloshing pail of sudding water, amble past. The manhole cover behind emits a series of receding bangs as I approach where Via Farini meets Via D'Azeglio. A muscular young chap clatters out a table and covers it in tricolour-filled posters for the coming local elections. The owner of the *tabacchi* opposite steps out, runs a hand through his white hair and frowns at this man, whom I guess is of a different political persuasion. Another, far more feeble fellow approaches, bent backed and toothless, with a piece of card before his chest covered in red writing I am unable to read, his cupped hand out before him, but when our eyes meet he turns suddenly away, seeing perhaps a lack of congeniality in my face.

I cross the throbbing roadway to the Palazzo Legnani, its front gate wide open, revealing at either side of the sylvan courtyard two centaurs silently gesturing to each other. On the street behind revs a bus after a car after a moped after a coupé, all throwing dust and exhaust into the air, while before me appear shining shop windows filled with eyeless mannequins. The terrazzo under my feet alters into planes of the most pristine marble, as overhead the walkway ceilings morph into tall arches as finely detailed as any aisle in any church in any city. The frescos, sky blue, show the faces of patrons and the most delicate of birds stalled in symmetrical flight, circled by dismembered cherub's heads, all disappearing around the corner as I step down into the plant-covered Piazza Cavour, an undulating space shaded with handsome trees, while its lowlands, as it were, are dotted with people and covered over with shrubs, grasses, a subtle fountain – water sprouting from a rock – a granite plinth, a copper statue of a seated man, a flamingo bent sipping from a pool, all of which is now enveloped in a warped blanket of rasping from the cicadas in the trees.

On the far side of Via Garibaldi, the shade of a tiny alley-way opens up to me and I make for a café I have not been in for years. I used to sit outside of this Caffè Rinaldi and read from the pink pages of the *Gazzetta dello Sport*, circling unknown words as I slowly improved my Italian.

I can see through the window three men at the far counter. As I enter, they turn, then turn back.

They seem to be exactly a generation apart, and stand along the sunlit bar like ascending notes on a scale, all three now leaning into their espressos, blowing the tendrils of rising steam aside before they each take a gulp and replace their cups onto their saucers with chaotic tinkles of ceramic and steel.

'*Aqua*,' I croak to the owner, who is leaning, arms crossed, on the far end of the bar.

'*Naturale o frizzante?*'

'*Naturale*,' I call.

Over the lottery machine, covered in yellow and white paper slips, he hands me a cool bottle of water, and like a colonialist having just emerged from a desert adventure, I drink down the bottle to its end.

'*Che caldo.*'

To which this owner, a local man of thinning grey hair and a nose more youthfully aquiline than his years, and who it seems has seen days far hotter than this before, merely shrugs.

I pause a moment, looking at the empty bottle, and it occurs to me that I will need to ask Bernadette how it is she prays, and the idea of this then fills me with a feeling of disquiet.

I pay up as the three men file out the door, each bidding the owner farewell.

The heat is beating down on Via Garibaldi. I look back over my shoulder at Piazza Cavour in the distance as the Bank of Italy looms above – its corners, capitals and frieze covered in white netting, while the park, as far as I can see, is reduced to mere towers of shining green punctuated in its gut with a blazing bush of brightest pink.

The street then opens out into a square leading up to the ancient red-bricked Basilica of Saint Dominic, and stepping into the shadow of a statue of this saint perched up high on a column of copper and stone, I see he brandishes with his left hand an enormous lily. Pushing more sweat from my brow, I look on at the sun's rays streaming out from behind his darkened head and body, his right arm, meanwhile, raised, as if to hold back the sky.

5

WAVES OF FABRIC

On the other side of the towering cool of the basilica glows a lone white bust of Saint Dominic. He gazes up at some clouds passing beyond a window shining blue in the dome way above.

In the surrounding hush, I bend and look closely at Saint Dominic's impassive face, and such is the brightness across his high cheekbones that, for a moment, I believe a tear from his left eye has spilled across his skin.

Philomena told me one morning some years ago, when we were passing this basilica on our way to the weekly market in town, that this bust was made, just after the war, to the dimensions of the head and shoulders of the saint, all taken from a scan, she said, of the saint's remains. She told me she'd been learning about 'all of this stuff' in school and that she'd like to maybe study history when she got older. I remember saying that this was probably a good idea. It was around then, when she was fourteen or so, that she began confiding in me more. She'd fallen out with her father, Stefano, a durable, intelligent man, who I have met only a handful of times. And this falling-out led to Philomena speaking to me more often, and I liked her company then very much. She made up with her father, but our small friendship still grew into this easy thing that I think both of us now enjoy.

She likes when I talk about my time, years ago, learning to sculpt stone in Utrecht, and this often leads me to Anna. When Philomena met Anna, she was still young, and she asked Anna if Patricia was her sister. To this, Anna just laughed and said, 'Oh, she's my twin sister,' and then she grinned, putting her arm around me. 'And John, here – he's my younger brother! We're an odd old family, aren't we, dear Philomena?' A few months later, Anna came up again in conversation, during a meal, and I told Philomena that Anna's parents and her only brother no longer spoke to her because of the fact that Anna prefers the company of women to men. Philomena was troubled by this for days – the idea of Anna's family pushing her away for such a thing. The earnest downheartedness of her response at first surprised me and I felt stupid for saying so much, but it told me how sensitive Philomena is and I realise that this sensitivity has not since turned inward into self-preservation, but outward into a kind of thoughtfulness she shares with her mother. There's a photograph of Philomena that sits on the mantelpiece in our sitting room. She is standing beneath a lemon tree bathed in what looks like late summer sun. A pale line of reflected light arrows through the top of the tree, illuminating the leaves into tongues of white. Philomena is no more than six or seven, and her father, partly obscured by the tree trunk, is shaking the lemon tree. From above rain down countless lemons, all mere dabs of plummeting yellow in the photograph, and in amid all of this chaos stands Philomena in a red tracksuit. I could never tell if her face was scrunched up in fear or joy. It's a photograph that still makes me feel like an outsider in the place in which I live and an outsider to the two people I have most come to know. Beside this photograph stands a tiny bronze version of Achim and Bettina, a casting made by Bernadette as a surprise gift to me for my fiftieth birthday. I'd brought the plaster miniature I'd made back with me to Italy after Bernadette and I had emptied my apartment in Ireland for good. I then gifted it to Bernadette upon our return. Then, some weeks before my birthday, she'd made a silicon copy of it and brought it to a local workshop to be cast in bronze. She'd damaged the plaster version I'd made while making the copy, though – both heads had come free – and it had to be thrown away.

Taking the broad blonde steps up to the altar of the chapel, I approach an ornate white sarcophagus wherein they retain this saint's headless body.

A breeze whips up, wavering the leaves of monstera plants, and I stifle a sneeze. A young monk, dressed in cream robes, ascends the altar and veers around the marble tomb, it covered in symmetrical reliefs and doll-like sculptures all representing saints of importance to Bologna and Saint Dominic's tale. The monk comes to a halt and I notice he is standing next to the tiny marble figure of Saint Petronius, the patron saint of Bologna, who is always shown with the city in his hands, as if some greater entity put a model of the place there for him to perpetually present. Bernadette once told me, with an unusual show of local pride, that this part of the tomb was sculpted by 'the great Michelangelo'. As the young monk steps away, I advance towards this tiny white saint and take in the walled city in his hands, the droop of fabric below his wrists, his solemn inch-high face, his pointed mitre, his tiny toes. Then I look at the folds in his clothes and compare them to the ripples of fabric in the other three holy figures. The unnatural creases and counter-waves of fabric carved expertly onto this small figure all suggest to me that Saint Petronius's skin underneath his robe squirms with eels. I imagine if one of these eels were suddenly to move against his skin that this would surely make him twitch, and surely this would then force the city of Bologna, with its stacks and stacks of dried-clay bricks all so safely in his hands, to topple.

The young monk traverses the basilica and steps up into the Rosary of Marian chapel, where he genuflects at a small tree of winking candles. As I go to follow him, the great tower bell peals outside.

Looking up, I see a golden chandelier holding three red candles. It dangles from a shimmering chain arrowing up into the hands of a goat-faced cherub perched way up on a cornice, as if he were a grimacing miner dropping three flickering canaries into a shaft. Two bells sound outside and, as they fall into and out of resonance, I look once more at this cherub, now smiling broadly from this outcrop of white flowers.

I sneeze. Then, more ferociously, sneeze again.

I cross to the Rosary of Marian chapel, where I take in the strange daytime gleam of the space. I close my eyes and bow my head once more; then, I decide to leave as the rhythmic murmurings of a rosary emerge as if from the ground, and, suddenly and horribly short of breath, I return outside to the livid stones of the cobbled square where sit three women dressed in white, their red headscarves ruffling to a warm breeze.

I ask an ancient lady leaning into the cool of the darkening narthex what time it is, and, when she informs me of the hour, I realise that Philomena and Bernadette are probably already waiting for me at the *osteria*.

6

AMONG THE PINE TREES TO
THE REAR OF A BASILICA

A dark slant of shadow drapes itself across the upper edges of Via Urbana. Towards the end of the portico I see patches of shining terrazzo and square tables covered over in crisp white cloths, with stubby wine glasses twinkling translucently atop. Bernadette and Philomena sit at the furthermost table. Bernadette has her hair up and she is scanning a large plastic menu. Then she sees me arriving, narrows her eyes over the menu comically and begins to laugh. Philomena looks up too, waves and puts her phone face down onto the table. I give them both a kiss on the cheek, but Bernadette's eyes linger on me. She can tell there's something amiss.

'Hungry?' I ask Philomena.

'Very,' she replies. 'I had to skip breakfast; I slept in till eight! I was in bed last night much earlier than you two, though …'

Bernadette looks to her, then me, then smirks at us both, before she peers up at Signore Pastole, the owner of the *osteria*, emerging from the double doors. He is a robust and affable man, balding, in his mid-sixties, and he usually has a cigarette, lit or unlit, between his lips. Today, it is unlit.

Bernadette extends her hand to him and says, '*Ciao, Carlo*,' and to this he leans forward, pulls the cigarette from his mouth, takes her hand and gives her a kiss on her cheek. With a slight limp, he makes his way over to Philomena, and she, leaning up towards him, also receives a kiss on the cheek, and then he comes to me.

'Mr John!' he exclaims, and claps a hand upon my shoulder. '*I Tedeschi*,' he says, opening his arms; then, he utters, '*Bueno*,' to no one in particular.

He brushes the tabletop with his fingers, then fixes a crease on his serving apron and pulls a small notepad from his pocket as his body lifts an increment.

Bernadette, who always overeats when she is in any way hung-over or tired, orders a starter – the saltiest thing on the menu, a large portion of breadcrumbed Ascoli olives. Philomena and I can guess that we will be offered none of them, so we look to each other and order a small portion for ourselves to share. Then we all agree on a shared main – a platter of fresh fish and roasted vegetables – and with it a small carafe of the house white, a Pignoletto that comes from a family vineyard halfway up the hills beyond our house, and then we sit back and await the water and the bread.

A car passes with music thumping from its windows. An elderly woman with recently pomaded white hair shuffles past on the terrazzo behind, with many bags of designer clothing hanging from her tiny arms.

'How's work?' I ask Philomena, to which she shrugs, as her phone then dings.

I put my hand onto Bernadette's, which is resting on the arm of her chair, and she looks to me as Philomena informs us that it's a message from Henry, saying that he cannot join us. She returns her phone to the table and tells me that the morning at work was quiet.

'So, instead,' she says, 'I drafted my pre-application for that MA in Trieste ... And how was your birthday?' she continues, while pushing with her finger a strand of her fine dark hair from off her brow.

'The best,' I say, and her phone dings once more and Philomena brings the base of it to her ear, listening carefully to a voice message. I can hear Henry's clipped Bostonian twang from the phone.

I think of Anna, and the last time she might have eaten.

Bernadette then puts her other hand onto mine and looks to me, but I struggle to look back, for fear that I might begin to tear up.

'Tired?' she asks.

'A little,' I say, looking to the ground, and I realise that I don't want to mention Anna's plight in front of Philomena, not at lunch, not at this time of day. I can tell that Philomena became fond of Anna, during her stay. And, in any case, whenever we three eat together in public, we tend to end up speaking in Italian, and I don't want to relay this kind of news to her in a tongue that is still somewhat ungainly to me. There are times when we are together and I'm not wholly sure what language to speak to them in, especially if I want

145

to bring up clearly a serious issue, or if I've heard something awful on the news, but this time, today, I am sure I do not want to speak in my clumsy Italian about Anna's demise.

Signore Pastole appears behind me with a bottle of water, a carafe of white wine and a basket of circular flatbreads. Philomena leans forward, smiling, her hand outstretched towards the basket.

After lunch, we slump in our chairs for a while in the growing heat – all of us food-sated, dazed almost. The shining streets here at this time of year and at this time of day become viscously slow.

The roofs up beyond the porticos seem to shiver in the sun.

We say nothing to each other until Philomena rises and makes to offer us money for lunch, which Bernadette motions away. I think she likes that Philomena at least offers. Sometimes when Philomena stands up from the dinner table I marvel at how tall she has become. She is more athletic than elegant, and there is an economy in her movements that she does not share with Bernadette at all. Bernadette's movements, and especially her unselfconscious hand gestures, have an almost rococo flourish to them by comparison. Sometimes, when she is on the phone, I simply watch Bernadette's free hand and it is as if it is searching for some meaning in some space way beyond the words she utters. The thought of that hand ever being stilled fills me with pain.

As Philomena waves, then strides off around the corner and back into the sun, I can feel my eyes begin to tire and water.

Bernadette leans towards me and asks me what is the matter.

I tell her about my letter from Patricia, Anna's dire state and her request for me to pray for her speedy passing.

Bernadette sits back.

'Oh,' she says, putting her fingers to her lips. Her eyes soften, as she pushes a strand of hair behind her ear.

We sit quietly a while, as the table at the far end noisily vacates.

Signore Pastole reappears; then, with a gentle cough, disappears back inside.

Bernadette puts her hands onto mine, and squeezes.

After some moments staring at the dark terrazzo below, I look up, and ask Bernadette if she would consider helping me to pray.

She begins to laugh; then, she looks to me in something like shock.

We pay up; then, together, we make our way down Via Urbana and return to the cicadas calling in the warping afternoon heat.

Bernadette leads me across the road to a small park behind the apse of the basilica, and up to a bench, where we sit in the shade.

She tells me that she used to come here when she was young to try to picture her father. She says that this kind of quiet space might help me too.

I describe to her the intensity with which my mother ground her teeth that night she came back from the grotto, after she had had her holy vision, and I say that, since then, I have associated this awful noise, this motion with the task of praying.

Bernadette looks to me and then says, 'So, you never pray?'

I shake my head. 'It has only done damage, as far as I can see.'

Then I ask her how it is that she prays, and what is it that she sees, and does she hear anything at all? But she just carefully shakes her head and then closes her eyes to the sun.

We sit in silence for a while. I look up at a bird leaving a tree for the sky, where, in the white-blue, it swerves over and back before returning with a diving rustle to another tree mere metres away.

Bernadette opens her eyes. Her pupils have dilated enormously, as if two boulders have plummeted into two pools of blue, and I know, in the moments since she last saw me, she has been elsewhere.

I ask her to tell me what she sees when she closes her eyes to prayer, or, if she sees nothing, then to what it is she directs her blindness.

She looks at me almost in disappointment.

'That place,' she says, 'is only for me, John.'

I look to her, and then over to the pine trees above, waving their shadows upon the rear wall of the basilica.

Bernadette's face hardens into a thought and she says, 'If you are afraid to pray, then maybe Anna is better off without you.'

She lifts her hands from mine.

Then, not out of anger, or even pity, but a sort of inner, heatless disgust, she stands and asks, her palms open at her sides, 'How can you be on this Earth in this way?'

My eyes drop from hers.

At this, she turns and makes off towards the curve of the apse.

'I'll pray for Anna, John, of course, but I'm going home now,' she says over her shoulder. 'Come back whenever you feel you are ready.'

She disappears beyond the shrubs and trees.

I sit there a while in the heat and listen to the endless maraca-like chirping of the cicadas.

I stand and decide to make for Piazza Minghetti in the middle of town, following a route I once traced here, a year or so after I arrived, of the underground river – l'Áposa – as it winds its subterranean route under the streets of Bologna and on out into the open and undulating Emilia-Romagna countryside. If I follow the water, it might lead me to somewhere fecund and of use.

7

L'APOSA

Descending the narrow and cool Vicolo Dello Orto, I come upon a man trowelling cement into the side of a tall archway, through which I can hear a person snore.

From a window above billow two sheets of the most delicate white netting, and I recall from somewhere, long gone, the word *reticolato*. I stand a while, looking up at this dancing fabric, and, pushing more beads of sweat from my brow, I think of Anna and how her feelings for me sought only to hold me, or what was of me at that time, together, and to help keep me sufficient and distinct. I try for a moment to picture into what sort of dark within dark she must now be plunging as she falls away from this world of absence. Then, I realise that she could already be gone and not plunging anywhere at all, but merely lying with increasing stiffness on a bed, as people whisper around her. And yet …

I realise that I do not want to die here in this country, surrounded by these good people, whispering words around enlarging silences, of which, as my faculties fail, I will understand more and more. But it strikes me that I have no idea how I might go about arranging an alternative. I picture

4

myself sneaking beyond these city walls at night and making for the sea to stow myself away into a laden frigate of bloated sail, pointed towards the shores of home.

I look to my phone, forgetting that the battery is now done.

The workman, who has finished up his trowelling, passes me with a nod. He enters a courtyard filled with cypresses and narrow windows, all sullenly closed over to the heat.

At the street's end, I pass a woman walking a schnauzer as she talks into her phone. Then I am met with a reflective pane of glass displaying me, from head to foot, to me.

Fifty-six years and one day, and I look wholly bewildered.

I move off as a Vespa speeds by, dousing me in fumes. I feel a growing cool beneath my feet as I go, and I can tell that I have rejoined the route of the river below.

Like a giant reverse 'C', the Via Carteglioni bends in an even, light-filled curve up towards Piazza Menghetti. If the columns and arches leaned inward on Via Saragozza, here they sway outward, listing and ready to topple onto the empty street below. I make my way along the smooth terrazzo, past palatial furniture shops, empty convenience stores and a laneway leading to a café fronted with white seating brightened by the sun, where slumps a woman in a plastic chair, exhausted, her head lying in her arms, her dark hair draped out in waves across the table's surface.

An empty bus thunders past, revealing, as I turn, a huge building of alabaster stone.

In the centre of the piazza stands the bronze Minghetti, hat in hand, while gesturing imploringly at a long-disappeared crowd. A pigeon alights from his head with a clatter of wings and makes for the tip of a nearby flagpole, while beyond Minghetti's stone plinth gather four men in hi-vis vests, all calling one after another into a cross-shaped hole. I look through their legs, down onto this passing river, which I have not seen in the flesh before. The men turn to me, then turn back, as a colleague, in shining waders, steps breathless and dripping into the sun.

Standing there a while, I picture Bernadette leaving the old-town walls and making for the hill to home. She always spoke about how much she liked Anna and Patricia, and I wonder if she is now most reckoning with Anna's or Patricia's pain, and will she see, like me, that, as one fades, the other will be forced to grow. It then occurs to me that, if I can perhaps find a place of suitable darkness, then it is in such surrounds that I might find a state of prayer into which my mind can relent.

I turn from this underground rope of river and, as I pass the Café de Paris, an opening ribbon of dark birds squawk overhead. Then the two tilting brick towers, *Le due Torri*, way up at the main confluence in the city, loom into view, their shadows thrown, like premonitions of their collapse, across the rumbling red-roofed buildings to the north.

I pass Giusti's drapery, before entering a narrow street that narrows further as I go. The rising red and yellow buildings cantilever out either side, their walls almost touching. Out of this, the broad cobbled Piazza San Stefano blooms with its echoing array of restaurants and bars, dotted out with giant white parasols, like gloved hands, hovering over tables and chairs, which are filled with chatting tourists and restless locals. Beyond then emerges, from barely above the ground, a complex of brooding stone buildings with a tower pinwheeling behind.

Along the portico on the northern edge of this piazza I walk, the slabs of shining terrazzo below altering in bands of colour and texture as I go, and I imagine myself being transported down in a clanking open-walled lift, looking on at the layers of minerals and soil as I descend.

Metamorphic rock I: Hornfels
Grain size: fine
Main minerals: mica, quartz, clays
Structure: cleaved
Strength: very strong
Breaking pattern: fissile, brittle

8

WALTER

Fragrant green plants wave and rattle from behind an iron railing leading me into Via Gerusalemme, a strange and narrow street with large words of graffiti daubed violently all over its walls.

From a broad door stomps out a man pushing a wheelbarrow full of plaster and bricks. He is covered in white dust, and when I pass the entrance, I see a corridor, a sitting room, then a kitchen with no rear wall, and, beyond, there flaps and floats a sheet of shining tarpaulin above a small garden full of flowers.

A young woman, reclining on a bench and drinking a beer, smokes meagrely from an e-cigarette. As I sit at a table opposite, a slight young man comes out to take my order – a small glass of red wine. A tiny rubbish-truck bumps past, drawing behind it the stench of rotting food. After it passes, I spy, along a downpipe running from the roof of this bar, these words written in pink marker: *Non ho imparanto niente*, I have not learned anything. Three men take their seats a table over, one of whom nods, lifting an eyebrow at the barman delivering my wine. I take a drink and feel the liquid splashing down my throat as the eldest man of the three enters into what becomes a long and unbroken monologue, his right hand beating out the syllables. He wears a navy cotton beret and black-rimmed glasses, and appears thirty years older than the others, both of whom I would guess are in their forties.

The man who was wheeling the barrow a minute ago bumps past, now with his phone to his ear. From his shoulders collapse puffs of plaster.

There was a photograph of my father that I saw when I was young, on the front page of the local newspaper, the week after his first major accident at the quarry. It showed him bloodied, dazed and covered in dust, and being carried by three men towards an ambulance. He had taken a fall that day from a broad and often-used outcrop of stone. His fall stemmed from a moment of dizziness. On the second Thursday of each month, my father would usually call my mother at four in the afternoon to remind her of the monthly blast at this limestone quarry, which was about half a mile, as the crow flies, from our house. Then my mother would tell me to step away from the windows and into the jamb of one of the kitchen doors in our old bungalow, and we'd wait for the distant thud of an explosion. A few moments later, there would arrive the inevitable window-shaking tremors. I remember my mother calling to me from across the kitchen each time these tremors struck: 'That's just Father saying hello, John!'

On the afternoon of his accident, he did not come home, though, and he did not return for a month, and by that time he seemed to me altered, lessened and turned inward, or at least turned away. Some time afterwards, we moved from our bungalow and into an apartment in town, and my mother took on a second job as a cleaner in a local solicitors' office. I realise my father enjoyed his work – cutting large shards of stone free of a hill – and I reckon the pain he felt from not being able to carry it out hurt him as much as the seeming indignity he took from reducing our circumstances and over-burdening my struggling mother. And I realise, while sitting here on this timber bench in a narrow street in Bologna, decades later, that turning away from those who happen to be on this Earth with you, and who happen to love you too, is one of the worst crimes, and yet, I understand why my father disappeared from us in this way.

As I finish my drink and am about to pay, I see, wandering up towards me, Walter, a Nigerian man I've come to know. He's one of dozens of vendors that walk the city streets every day, selling LED lamps, cigarette lighters, joke glasses and such. Festooned with his rattling goods, he greets me with a smile.

'John,' he says, his arms held wide.

To which I greet him with a handshake, and, while grasping his hand, I pull myself from my seat and I can feel for a moment the lovely scale of his counterweight.

He asks me how my day is going.

'Very well,' I reply.

'Bravo,' he says, unconvinced.

The owner of the bar steps out and gives Walter a look that seems to tell him that he ought not to linger long.

'All OK with you?' I ask.

He shrugs; then, remembering something, he smiles. 'My girl, she's leaving for university next month,' he says.

'Where to?' I ask.

'A scholarship,' he replies. 'She's going to Milan!'

'Wish her my best. What is her name?'

'Alessandra,' he replies.

'You'll be lonely,' I say.

'I shall be,' he says, now smiling broadly, as if this loneliness will be to him a mark of her success. 'And you?' he asks once more. 'How are you today?'

'Lost,' I say. 'I've lost a friend.'

And he looks to me, but I look away.

Then, breaking the silence, I ask, 'Do you pray, Walter?'

He stalls a moment and then replies, 'All of the time.'

'Where?' I ask.

'Here, while I walk the streets,' he replies, pointing to his sandalled feet.

'And what do you think about?' I ask. 'What do you see?'

'My home, my parents,' he says. 'My maker.'

I look down and shake my head. I feel suddenly adrift of him.

Then he opens out his arms, but I refuse to take them.

'Maybe next time, Walter,' I say, averting my eyes. 'I don't know what would happen if you helped me now,' I say. 'But next time, Walter, feel free to help me then.'

We bid each other farewell and I walk to the end of the street, then I cross a small crumbling piazza and continue on past archways and courtyards filled with shining trees and singing youths; then, perspiring heavily again, I slow.

9

A BLOOMING CAPITAL

Out of a double doorway I can hear what sounds like a cello playing to a violin.

I look down through a corridor at a horseshoe of musicians to the rear of a bright inner courtyard. Rows of people listen to the rising and ornate falling of the tune.

As I step in, the riches of this music bounce from the walls and glide up off the galaxies of terrazzo flooring, all doubling and tripling each sound as I go, until the bass notes seem to fall deeper, then suddenly they gather up into the undersides of the lowest of the treble lines, where they adhere like pollen to the legs of soaring bees, detach, then tumble away. The musicians, all wearing black, lean and fidget in the distance while the baroque composition now empties itself skyward. I enter this inner courtyard as sunlight threads through a passing cloud. Lamps clink on overhead as a miasma of dust floats above the gravel. I return up the corridor, leaving this music behind. Then, before the main entrance door, I notice a set of stone steps leading down into a cellar from which echoes the sound of a single voice. I look about a moment, then I descend into a spiral of darkness until I find myself in a softly lit space, filled with squat stone arches.

I enter and take a seat.

To my left, flickers a candle with a flame so long it seems as if it is being stretched, lifted by an invisible thread, towards the surface of a pool of water far above me, and behind this flame leans a watercolour of a man I recognise as Padre Pio. I look around at the stone arches, sitting upon these fat mimosa columns, and for a moment, in this uncanny light, it seems as if the columns are themselves fountains sprouting stone in perfect gravity-led arcs, one onto another. Beneath an empty alcove in a dark corner sways a lone white plant. I stare at it a while. Then, looking downwards, that moment from years ago returns to mind, when that young medic cut off my football sock and released my splintered shin pad to reveal, thrusting through a large rip in my skin, the lower half of my tibia, it gleaming white while from it sprouted, like arcs of sputum pushed out through teeth, delicate spurts of blood issuing from a severed vein. I remember the contorted ashen face of this young medic looking on, hands wavering, at this strange contraption of blood and bone unwinding uncontrollably before him.

When I returned from hospital, a month later, my mother told me that she had prayed for me each day to Padre Pio. I realise she must have been praying for my gravely ill father as much as for me. I remember pleading with her not to. I knew how her praying loosened out her mind and her ability to resist its collapse. I look up and seek out the white plant beneath the alcove, but it seems to have suffused itself into the dark. I look back at Padre Pio's smiling face in this painting, his bandaged hands, his depicted beads, then I look around at these stone-spilling columns and, before I am taken in panic picturing my shinbone suddenly missing from below the knee, I stumble from this crypt, my right leg seizing up, and make instead for a door that leads me into dark, then shining, then darker cellars that seem to unspool subterraneously from each other, but, with the compaction of time in each stalled stone flourish in every corner and niche I encounter, I am forced back into the main crypt, past a naff and ancient papier-mâché pietà, up a broadening set of stone steps and out a large door into the light and air, where I stand a moment on the cobbled street to steady my breath. Then, I bend and roll up my trouser leg to inspect my shin, where I find a line of blood rolling down the skin. I pull the trouser leg up towards my knee, where lies an abrasion, which I stem for minutes with my fingers.

I slump to the ground, peering around, and I note that I've rejoined the same piazza I was in before, but now on the adjacent flank, and I spy in the shadows of the trees in the middle of this place dozens of figures lying and looking at their phones, and I recognise these persons as those from the huge Parc Dello Montagnola, where they drift around each day, whistling and ticking while calling out their wares to those in need of a fix.

I roll my trouser leg back down and stand.

Then, as a small white car rushes past, I hear from below its chassis a clump.

A pigeon lies there on the cobbles lifting its head from its chest, filthy and decrepit – its head and wings streaked through with the strangest of blonde fibres, neither hair nor feather. It is untouchable, but unbloodied. A rubbish truck turns onto the street, so I shoo this bird towards the footpath. It hops then waddles towards a crevice between two blue marble wall plates, where it lies down with a ruffle in the shade. I make my way up towards Via Vitale, where I turn into the sun and continue on for some distance, the terrazzo altering again below me, but the slabs here have dates written on them with tiny interlinked fragments of white stone.

Metamorphic rock II: Gneiss
Grain size: coarse
Main minerals: quartz, mica, feldspar
Structure: foliation
Strength: strong
Breaking pattern: irregular

As my breathing becomes less laboured, I see before me, in a length of sun-checkered portico, a tiny door.

My walking has by now slowed into what might appear like caution.

I push the door and enter, and up above and all around me extends in vaulting planes the cool darkness of Chiesa San Vitale y Agricole. Bernadette once told me that her uncle Francisco churches here every week, and, though I had always resolved to visit Francisco's place of prayer, I never got to it, and yet, here I am at last, and I realise that I am now wholly parched.

The church is empty except for four men in dark-brown robes, in a line just short of the altar. It's so quiet that it seems the place itself has somehow become aware of me and my intention: to pray here for the death of my friend. I bless myself and make towards the left of the nave.

Incense twists upward from an altar urn in front of a lone monstera plant, itself in front of a white, cloth-draped table, behind which towers a dark oil painting depicting the violent deaths of these two local saints.

The four young monks drop to their knees with their heads bowed low, almost touching the floor. I look with envy at the seeming ease of their supplication.

Soon, a sort of stillness comes over them – four rocks on the shore of a vast waterless lake. I peer around, taking in the sculptural flourishes bound up in the iconography. Beams of secret light fall across the upper edges of the altar walls and bounce and dissipate onto us citizens below. Apart from the silently twisting smoke, nothing moves. It is as if the whole edifice is now stunned into stasis as it looks on at this slender column of fragrant smoke. Then, way up to my right, over the shoulder of a sculpture of San Vitale appears the tiny head of a monkey. It clambers onto the saint's head and perches there a while, its tail falling in a loop around San Vitale's ear. It has golden fur and a dark and thoughtful face. It seems to be one of those small golden langur monkeys. I look to the monks and around the church, to see if anyone else has seen this too, but all I can sense is the prayers being whispered by these four folded men. The monkey, sitting insolently on San Vitale's head, lifts its hairy hands to its ears and grimaces. Then he disappears behind the statue of the saint. I stand and walk towards the altar to see where this monkey has gone. But, before I've passed the urn of incense, I feel a hand grasp my shoulder. It is the most senior of the monks telling me that I cannot approach the altar during adoration. I nod, then take my seat once more, scanning the altar, the apse, the sculptures and reliefs for any sign of this young golden langur monkey. A leaf falls through a shaft of early evening light. It sails down in giant esses. I follow the leaf-trail back up to the top of a column, its capital now sprouting in the umbrage not stucco acanthus leaves but green and yellow flowers. I look on at this blooming column. Then I look at these four monks bent in deep and medita-tive prayer. I look up once more and see a pink petal now fall from the lustrous column capital. I rub my eyes; I blink. I close my eyes for some moments, then I rise and leave without looking again at the sculpture of San Vitale or the monks or the head of that flourishing column. I think, as I step down the nave towards the entrance and the carriage-way outside, that perhaps the base of this column sits over a section of the underground river, l'Áposa, and perhaps the centre of the column has returned to an osmosis-enabling clay, ripening the leafy capitals.

10

SEEMINGLY MYSTICAL PLANES

Emerging from a daze, I'm met by a barrage of cicadas' chirrups, an ambulance speeding by, a flare of sun and a red open-topped bus blaring music.

I find myself on a thoroughfare I recognise from the first Halloween night I spent in this city, and I recall how amazed I was by this place, walking from its streets into its dark high churches.

Bernadette and Philomena were in Naples then, visiting Bernadette's sister, Louisa, so I felt alone and less inhibited, and this extended to my feelings in the city that night. I savoured stepping across each threshold, from the rush of traffic on the street and into these cavernous spaces full of candles, shadows and seemingly motionless people. The ease with which I could traverse these two spaces – inside and outside, noisy and quiet – seemed that night to upturn the reverence I always had from when I was young and approaching church, the building on the hill that was only ever visited at industrially fixed times of the week. And I realise, as I walk up this Via Zamboni, with the smoky and cacophonous traffic congealing to my right, that none of these churches I've visited today quite suit the daylight, because the shining surfaces of these places have blurred any thoughts I might've developed about the spaces behind the colour and sheen, the important spaces where the shadows might grow and develop peaceful structures in the darker corners of my mind and away from these anxious rockfalls.

The evening here is still bright and hot, and though the stark brilliance of the summer has long passed, I realise it will not be dark for many hours.

In a yellow colonnaded length of otherwise unmarked wall appears a tiny servants' entrance. The moment I step in, I realise I'm back at one of those churches from my first breathtaking Halloween in Bologna, and I realise too that I have not been in this vast *chiesa* at any time in the ten years since. It looks as though someone has come into the place and polished every painting, sculpture, relief, column, capital, candlestick ... It is, in short, ablaze.

Taking a seat on a wooden stool in a rhombus of light, I think – looking around at this bizarre palace – of the church I saw one morning with a friend, Marcus, an English film-maker who has long since moved back to his home town of Lincoln. He was here for a number of years on a sabbatical from film-making. He had begun to work with a company that repaired facades. He always seemed far too manic a person to me for so sedate a job, until I realised that, to carry out his work on towers and church roofs, he and his colleagues would abseil daringly down and around these edifices with ropes, pulleys and winches. One weekday afternoon, he asked me if I'd like to join him 'on a small job' near to the middle of town. It was a decommissioned and bolted-up ex-*chiesa*, San Barbaziona, and he said he could give me a view of the whole thing from a window in the roof.

The following Saturday morning, we abseiled down from a tower crane in a neighbouring site to a small window too dirty to quite see through. Marcus stuck his boot through it and we watched the shards of glass spill like water through the empty nave below. We leaned in and there stood this church, stripped back to the bone, not a colour, not a brick, not a single piece of stucco or marble or steel – just this towering ribcage of dusty stone. It was like looking into the underside of a giant dog's mouth, and I pictured, as we swung there gently in the cool dawn air, the place being emptied of its relics and paintings and sculptures, then stripped by tiny workers of its planes of marble, with every stucco blossom gouged off the columns in a petty display of retrieving what was theirs.

Through the entrance to my left, a skinny white hound wanders in and begins to chase and bark around the nave. It barks and barks in growing echoes, until it is pursued by a determined young woman, broom in hand, out the door from which it came.

I look up at a frieze of stone saints gesturing at happenings in the seemingly mystical planes above, and I wonder how Marcus's life is going and if he is back making films again, or if he is nowadays still dangling from the sides of holy buildings, monitoring cracks and flaws. He told me, later that morning, as we drove through the twisting roads of northern Bologna, that, when he worked on any tall religious building here, he snipped 'as a small souvenir' a metre or so of the earthing rod that runs from the highest point in each building down to the ground. He wanted to see what would happen to these buildings if they were struck by lightning in a storm, but now with no route to take the energy to the ground. I think he envisioned great explosions all over the city on a night of heaving electricity. I picture a small vitrine in his home in Lincoln, with strips of conducting rod all sitting on tasselled cushions and, underneath, the names of churches in Bologna inscribed onto pieces of card.

I close my eyes, bend my head, and try to pray for Anna, but all I can hear in the distant dark is the nauseating sound of loosening rock, and then, as my chest tightens up once more, I see a large arm belonging to a huge religious statue in a basilica elsewhere in the city suddenly dislocating at the shoulder and plummeting to the ground, where it smashes into fragments, destroying the peace that had held the arm there in the first place for so long.

I raise my head and open my eyes as an elderly man shuffles towards me.

He is ringing a bell.

But I cannot quite hear it.

I widen my jaws to pop my ears, and in pours the sound of a pealing bell. This small stiff man, as he clears the church for the day, stops for a moment, turns and surveys the place. Then, he raises his hand as the lights over him go out and a section of the dome gaping above the altar falls into darkness. His hand quavers there a while, fingers spread, each digit shining out of the shadows of the dome, and it seems as if this hand is no longer gesturing in this world, but guiding, pushing some entity into another. He drops his hand and begins once more to ring his bell, shooing the visitors like farmyard geese towards the door. The sound of this hand bell bounces all over the church, creating a chaos of sound waves that seem, as I turn and walk towards the glowing narthex, to mimic the chaos of signals being emitted from the holy objects and images around me, and I hope as I traverse this huge room that in some places these waves of chaos will cancel themselves out into moments of silence.

I step out of the main entrance and into the sun.

I cup my hand over my brow and squint.

A stream of arrows arc through the city sky and disappear.

Across the square, I hear the cellos and violins still play.

I'm back again to where I was, not an hour ago, on the edge of Piazza Rossini, but on the outer realms of a new musical construction.

I touch my lips – now bone dry – and, as I make off towards a bar I know on Via Oberdan, I look to a bench at the centre of this square, where on one afternoon during Anna and Patricia's stay I was walking to meet them and bring them out for lunch, but instead what I came upon was a small Italian man, dressed in a three-piece suit, standing in front of their sunlit bench, berating them. Patricia stood and, with a few subtle but protective movements of her upper body, movements more like the ring generalship of a fistless fighter, she ushered this angry little man away and past the bench she and Anna were sharing, until he relented and disappeared, all slackening gesture, around a corner. Then Patricia sat back down beside Anna, and she put her arm around her, and Anna simply smiled. She reached forward, then, and gently patted Patricia's hand.

Metamorphic rock III: Marble
Grain size: fine to medium
Main minerals: calcite
Structure: crystalline
Strength: very strong to strong but brittle
Breaking pattern: cleavage

Across the busy carriageway, the Charcuterie Oberdan empties and fills with tourists and students. A hunched and elderly gentleman with curly white hair silently looks out at me from one of the niches beside the entrance. He drops a purpling curve of Parma ham into his mouth.

A waiter places a small glass onto my table.

He steps back, wordlessly, brandishing a bottle of white wine and a bottle of Chianti. I ask for the Chianti.

This waiter is bald and painfully thin. Then he tells me about the wine he has poured in a voice so gravelly it is as if, when he speaks, his mouth opens but the words come to me quietly from behind. I taste the wine and nod. He then pours me a fine glass of this watery-red wine, which, once he has stepped away, I gulp down in three mouthfuls.

I roll up my trouser leg and inspect my knee and shin once more. All is well; not even so much as a bruise. I roll the fabric down and sit back to take in the busy street.

When Bernadette and I brought Anna and Patricia here on the last day of their visit, I got talking to Anna about what she hoped to do upon retirement, but she just looked at me a while, her eyes shifting across my face. She then put her glass of water onto the tabletop and said that she didn't see it as retirement so much as the cessation of a career that was a complete waste of time. She told me that this restoration work she had engaged in for her life was little more than a camp posture of defiance in the face of a natural disintegration. We spent our time, she said, us fools, holding up waves of stone that only ever wanted to crash. She told me that building playgrounds was a far better use of my time.

The white dog I saw in the church chases from around a corner, still barking and lurching at everyone it meets. It looks as if it is desperately seeking its owner. Francisco's dog, Lupito, would often stay with Bernadette and me when we moved into our apartment on the hill – the one above his workshop. Lupito was a nervous sort and would station himself each day at the balcony railing, surveying for hours our street. Whenever an unfamiliar dog appeared on the roadway, over fifteen feet below, Lupito, unable to compute that it could not fly up and harm him, barked this dog, in an enlarging fear, away. Then, whenever Lupito saw Bernadette or Philomena or, heaven forbid, Francisco on the street below, he would rush headlong between the balcony and the back door of the apartment, yelping and whining and knocking furniture as he sped. And the longer I observed Lupito doing this, the better I began to picture his understanding of the house – a series of interlinked fields of intensity – and I began to see that, for him, the street below was, in some Piranesi-like way, connected on a direct plane of intensity to the back entrance of our first-floor apartment, and it was only then, when I began to imagine how he montaged reality, that his great fear of strangers below began to make more sense, and I stopped shouting at him whenever he emitted a sudden bark from the balcony to some unsuspecting dog and dog-owner passing on the street below.

As I pay and leave, a pigeon flies over my left shoulder, swooping as if it is being chased. Its reflection flits in the street's first-floor windows, as the reflection's reflection, then, in the windows opposite, flits once more. This wretched bird is halted mid-air as if it has met a sheet of glass. It veers right and settles onto a tie bar under an arch, where it stiffens and emits from its rear a dollop of faeces that smatters on the metal tie, then dissipates onto an angle of red *tenda* below.

I walk down the street for some time before turning onto the chaotic Via dell'Indipendenza, where, up ahead, bustles Paninocoteca, a small neon-lit café where Philomena and I meet most evenings for a snack or an espresso and a chat, before we push on home together, but now I walk past with my head down in fear that she might be there.

As I reach a set of steps leading up to an archway, my chest tightens horribly once more.

I pause and gather my breath.

I shake my head, then loosen out my left hand, clench it and continue through this dry late-summer heat to a shallow set of steps, a length of terrazzo and then a small wooden door, through which I step.

11

A BARE AND DESOLATE GROTTO

This giant church is wholly quiet, like the outer lobes of a sleeping brain, and I can sense that an evening Mass is about to take place at its head.

Along the lectern aisle I pass a line of towering columns, all leading to two confessionals flanking red marble pillars holding aloft a Roman arch, which frames at its centre a painting of Christ on Earth looking heavenward to his Father.

Entering the nave, I take a seat at the end of a pew. An old Bolognese lady at the other end is either asleep or deep in prayer.

Overhead span florid arches leading up to the altar – a theatre of marble steps, bright balusters and countless drapings of crimson cloth. Gigantic columns stand either side, flanked by four statues, all holy men whose names and stories I am unable to decode. I look at them a while, until the Carrara marble of these figures begins to de-crystallise into a rough old limestone and then I picture these figures of limestone disfiguring and crumbling into a torrent of water flowing towards a quarry filled with plummeting quarrymen. Two baroque balconies from above the nave slide into view, both built as if for a dictator or a queen to wave at their dear subjects far below. Daylight streams in from the windows above, as somewhere behind me a rumbling decade of the rosary completes its course, then, on the altar in the distance appears a priest, dressed in white robes, and with his arrival the whole place falls into calm.

During the opening hymn, a large crucifix lights up and hovers spectrally to the rear of the altar. Its wood has the strangest-seeming lustre. It shows a wide-eyed Christ upon the cross, while to his right awaits his mother and to his left Mary Magdalene. The Virgin Mother stands before a line of long-leafed plants waving around at her feet, as if she is about to step out into a vast pampas of unknowable dimensions. I look at the middle-aged and bespectacled priest once more. He brings his hands together as his voice reverberates around the nave, and I realise that the complexity of the decoration here contrasts almost to incoherence with the simple cruciform shape of the building, and I realise too that one of these aspects of the space – the larger – can be understood at a glance, whereas the other – the detail – is impossible to understand at all.

I peer over my shoulder at the huge rectangular window above the main entrance, shrouded now in a theatre-sized curtain of regal blue, and in this largeness it occurs to me that I am being shrunken by the scale of what surrounds me and, in shrinking me so, a place of this kind then surely makes the most banal of thoughts take on a profundity that the thoughts themselves have scarcely earned; and I wonder if this theatre of largeness is one that creates conditions not for deep prayer but merely the shrinking of original thought. And if this is so, I wonder, then, are arenas such as this not merely theatres to produce the hoax of deep feeling out of the warping of scale and the forgetting of the intimacy of adulation.

A flicker of light from across the nave flutters up my hands, my forearms, my chest. Then it disappears. It reappears, like a butterfly of white, and, as I look for its source, this flickering evening light meets my eyes. I raise my hand to it and this light flutters away and back and away and back, until I see from across the nave a boy of nine years or so. Alongside him sits an elderly woman whom I take to be his grandmother. As he flickers with a piece of mirror this light over my chest again, a smile playing across his lips, I decide to stand and go to a shaft of light of my own, this one falling across a row of anterior pews. The young boy's grandmother has taken out her rosary beads and has begun to pray. I produce my phone and reflect with its face a square of light back across the nave and onto this boy, until he detects it too. I wiggle the square of light about, then shine it onto his grandmother's mouth as she prays, the light spilling into the darkness from where her whispers emerge. Then, I shine my square of light along her cheek and into her ear. The boy looks up at her ear in a pose of kitsch devotion.

I put my hand over the face of my phone and sign out, in Morse code, the words:

-.... / --. --- --- -.. / - --- / -.-- --- ..- .-. / -- --- - .... .
.-. --..-- / ... --- -

be good to your mother, son

Her rosary beads rattle.

Then, as the grandmother nears the end of her first decade, I direct my square of light to the right of the altar. The young rascal looks to me. I nod my head towards the tiny square of light, which I've placed into the bosom of a buxom angel beside this altar, where the priest, arms spread, has now entered song. The young boy searches the angel, then with raised eyebrows he looks to me. I look away while leaving this wanton square of light – as if unbeknown to me – lying rudely in the cleft of the angel's bosom. The boy begins to snicker, then laughs, as do I. But the boy's laughter lasts only seconds before I hear his feet and those of his grandmother squeak upon the marble as she marches him down the nave, and I imagine them re-emerging out into the dry evening heat and this young boy receiving a telling off.

I put away my phone and wait until the sunshine I'm sitting in slides off. My breathing has eased, but my chest feels tight. I put my hand to the underside of my ribcage and close my eyes, and for some moments I see, far away, *Kritios Boy* still propped aloft on a metal plinth. I wonder if he or any of his incomplete roommates have moved an atom since I last saw him. I picture that mysterious swivel in his hips and it occurs to me that perhaps this posture was not him hesitating before stepping forward, but instead was him turning away from something – from a world of who? And why? And towards a world of how? And what? Or perhaps, I then think, it was him in the act of turning back once more, towards Jerusalem, to face again the world that he had in the first instance regretted leaving.

I enter the rosary chapel in the more padded shadows of this place, where now pools a lone huddle of about a dozen people. I look at the young priest leading this rosary, while up behind him stands a statue of the lonely Virgin Mother, not dissimilar in posture and scale to the statue of the Marian Virgin Mother from my childhood church.

I look at this figure and realise that, if I were to pray, it would be for this figure not to move, to give me no sign of life and to stay motionless forever. I think about my mother and her admissions of such sights, back long before such things were, by sheer numbers, made acceptable. It was a strangely adamant thing for her to do and, worse, to continue to insist on, and I realise that in her admitting to such a sight that she was being in essence perfectly disobedient. I wonder whether in the moment or moments that night when she first witnessed the statue moving in that grotto did she consider suppressing what she saw, what she would say, and whether she thought it might be better to tell no one at all about what she had witnessed and keep it to herself, and simply decide there and then, with a similar adamancy, never to peer at a holy figure again. I look on at the heft of ornamentation stacked around the statue of the Virgin Mother up high in the chapel before me – with these churchgoers arranged in front, heads all bent in murmured prayer – and I think how, in this directing of mass devotion towards the statue, it becomes somewhat hollowed out of life, and all of this ornamentation around it then acts merely as further insulation. I imagine that a statue of the Virgin Mother in a bare and desolate grotto near to my home town, on a cold wet night decades ago, must, in comparison, have seemed to my mother, through the dark and rain, to be filled with coursing currents of vinegar, piss and blood.

Then, I wonder what my mother was doing there at all.

Then, I think of Anna slowly vacating herself.

And I think of my Bernadette too.

I look up at the priest leading the rosary and then at the statue of the Virgin Mother over his head, her eyes cast skyward, and I imagine this small stage I'm looking at as a theatre with two actors – the priest entirely filling his role, whereas the statue of the Virgin Mother is empty of life, but indicating to a holy entity far away from the stage itself. And I visualise a triangulation between me, the statue of the Virgin Mother and the holy entity this statue represents. I name this triangular arrangement the 'theatre form of devotion', and I imagine this form of devotion as stable, untroubled and allowing for a life of easy faith, but then I envisage the entity of the Virgin Mother rushing in behind this statue and for a moment taking on her form and, for a briefer moment still, indicating to me through bodily movements of some secret kind that she can see me as much as I can see her, and in so doing, this arrangement then collapses from the stable triangulation of theatre into a fearful single line between the holy entity of the Virgin Mother and me, and I realise that, if this arrangement were to alter so, then it would alter from the form of theatre into the early breachings of reverence. And from this I then discern what is direct and frightful in any act of reverence, and by extension then what was not mad, but brave in my mother too.

I become aware that I am kneeling.

I look back to the priest as the rhythms of the rosary now enter what seems to me to be their last minutes-long waves of call and response. I sit and look around at this giant church once more, and, realising it is all still far too bright, I stand and make my way across to the other side of the nave, where I stall a while behind a marble column before stepping into and taking a seat in the central chamber of a stifling confessional.

I lean my head back against the mahogany wall and listen for the rosary outside to come to an end and for all of the priests, monks, nuns and the especially devout of this congregation to leave, bringing with them their squeaks and murmurs and creaks.

I sit here, pulling the second crimped sachet of electrolyte from my trouser pocket. I finger it a while and decide to close my eyes until the church, and its darkness, is mine.

12

COUNTERWEIGHT

After what must be two hours, and after what must be half an hour since the giant bells rang out above and the last door of this place closed over and locked, I step from the confessional box.

I round the marble column and the body of the basilica opens back up to me.

It seems much colder now. The whole place glints and tilts in the dark like a ship at night creaking across calm waters. I peer about for some moments before venturing towards the centre of the nave.

I pause in the shadows, then approach the altar and circle the pulpits, the suspended paschal candle and the tabernacle behind.

As my eyes adjust, the statue of the crucified Christ emerges from the dark. I look up at his painted eyes looking down at me. I step in behind the figures of the Virgin Mother and Mary Magdalene either side of him. I can smell the ancient tangy cedar off them all, and even though I know I should not touch something so old, I run my finger along Mary's shoulder. I look down over the whole church, the glowing transept, nave and the dark disappearing aisles. Much of what remains in this space has thrown itself into a darkness framed by greater darknesses, and in the falling quiet I can hear only the odd tick and the lowest thrum of what's left of what I assume to be the traffic outside. I listen more closely, but all I hear now is the distant gurgle of water. I step down towards the Gospel lectern and continue to the aisle. I pause at the side chapel where the rosary was taking place before I stowed myself away, and I lift a candle from a cloth-draped table and light it off another flickering near a golden crucifix standing at the feet of the statue of the Virgin Mother.

I walk around the church, into and out of its towers of shadows, leading myself with this single flame, it throwing what light it can onto the reliefs and columns and the frag-mented faces and tormented bodies of the sculptures and paintings around me.

I re-enter the nave and the candle implodes onto itself great warbling absences, a billowing architecture of umbrage that opens, wavers and closes as I go.

At the raised altar, I light the candles at the foot of the choir, and all of those around the Virgin Mother too. I take a seat at the head of the nave and try not to think of what is coming behind me, but only of what is available to see before me, and to this I hear an echoing squawk from far up to my right. I spy upon the metal halo of Saint Pietro two parrots. One has plumage full of colour, while the other plucks feath-ers from its chest and spits them out. The feathers drift down until they disappear into the darkness below. This dreadful bird is stripping its belly of colour and its beige and wrinkled skin shines wanly in the candlelight. The other bird swoops out a shallow arc high into the air above the altar. Then it descends and settles on the head of Mary Magdalene, its claws scraping across her crown. It sits there a while longer, then emits another echoing if toneless squawk. I look up to my left at the head of a column where from the capital now slowly blooms a green leaf, then another and another, then a flower of yellow, out of which emerges a great glistening curve of stamen. The other parrot squawks as it takes an uneasy flight across the nave, the altar and into the darkness of the apse behind, where, with another shriek, it disappears.

Walking back towards the front entrance of the basilica, away from this bird and this single blooming capital, I smell the damp of water all around and I imagine an unruly jungle river coursing down the broad carriageway outside.

I sneeze and, into its echo, I sneeze again.

At the door, I take out the sachet of electrolyte, rip it open and pour the powder into the holy-water font. I stir the contents with my finger, then I lift this hefty marble font from its casing and take a number of drinks.

With a small pool remaining, I return to the altar where the feathered parrot – blue, green, yellow – still perches insolently on the head of Mary Magdalene, its beady eyes taking a warped measure of its surrounds.

I leave the font down at the foot of the altar alongside a monstera plant. I step back to see if the parrot will be tempted towards this drink. I sit once more, looking up at the blooming column's capital, and notice it has stopped sprouting leaves and flowers and stamen and is instead now covered over in the most lush of bright green ferns whose fronds waver in an earthly breeze. The waddling parrot calls out three more of its demented shrieks. Then, at the bowl appears that golden langur monkey. It is surely the same one I noticed above those praying monks. He looks to me for many moments. Then he scampers forward, but I dare not move. He is a small animal, and yet, I am still wary of his strength and his irrationality. If he attacked, how could I reason with him to stay away from me, and I am not sure where I would run if I had to. He turns to the small marble font and with his tiny hands he hurriedly ladles this mineral-filled water up into his mouth, where glint his huge incisors and above them shine his blinking eyes. The bird calls once more, as if it has intuited that its less-feathered companion has travelled too far into the darkness of the apse behind and is lost forever. I look to the dangling green fronds of the fern, way up, then at the parrot, then at the monkey once more, who has by now stopped drinking and is staring back at me.

His lips close into a prehensile pout.

Then, he extends a finger and points to something in the darkness far behind me. But I, wary, dare not look; instead, I stare back across the choir and into the stilled eyes of this monkey, for some time, until the parrot screams again and, with this, the golden langur monkey scampers off into the apse behind the altar.

I stand and follow.

Stepping beyond the ancient sculpture of Christ, I begin towards this strange apse, out into which I proceed until the darkness closes so wholly in around me that I cannot with any certainty step forward.

I drop to my hands and knees and begin to crawl, feeling out with my fingers what is solid and worthy of my weight. As I crawl, I can feel my eyes adapting to this dark. Then, from a glimmer in the near distance I can make out the profile of this monkey. It clambers up something of considerable heft, but when I look up, I cannot see a thing. I consider turning back, but, because I now feel no fear, I realise there is no point in going back because if I arrive there I would have no idea from what I have returned. So I stand and step towards this thing the monkey clambered upon, and I realise it is either a tree or something built in the fashion of a tree. I feel around its surface, but I cannot discern its bark, its coating, so I step closer and sniff it, but it yields no smell I've smelt before, and so yields nothing for me with which to compare. I circle this thing with my left hand upon it.

Then, in the distance, a patch of light swims into view, and from it I hear the whistle of a bird. I walk through the dark towards this entity, and as I go I intuit more of these treelike things beside me and it occurs to me that if these things are built then there is likely something above them sheltering my route and that I am being led through hidden chambers connecting this basilica with another, and perhaps, with this waxy parrot and this monkey, I am being drawn around the most holy and ancient parts of Bologna. The monkey appears now in a frame of light before me. He is hunkered on the ground, looking into this bright chamber where sits a woman, Saint Cecilia, while beside her is seated a man of advanced age. She is silently unwrapping from her torso, hips and legs bandages, showing this companion her flesh, every inch of it disfigured and scalded and swollen and red. She runs a finger over it, pointing out the boils and places of particular damage. Then she bends her head forward, lifts her long hair to one side and reveals to this man, a doubter surely, the three papish axe-gouges down the back of her neck. The man, a frail looking chap, takes fright. He puts his trembling fingers to his lips as he looks at these deep wet gouges in her neck and these colonies of sores around her torso and legs. I step toward this room until it occurs to me that these people lie in a kind of daylight that seems to be casting two sets of shadows across the ground. I realise the illumination in here must be stemming from two sources of light of equal strength and I see too that Saint Cecilia's feet are immobile, fused together in their pose. I step closer once more into the edge of a magnetism I've not ever felt before – a magnetism that comes from some great silence that lies out in the rolling hills way beyond these two figures. But then, as I feel my centre of gravity tilt towards this quiet land, I hear the call of the parrot, far off, from where I came, and I am reminded of the altar, the choir, the transept, the nave and the world behind me of a single sun. Then, I feel Saint Cecilia's gaze. But I cannot dare to look. I sense her mouthing something to me from her chamber, which, if I were to guess, from these mouthed absences, is a request for me to return her gaze and for this she will offer me protection. I realise that these things she mouths, though facing away from language, still disintegrate meaningfully into the realm of silence.

I falter a moment; then, I hear her clear her throat.

But instead of returning her gaze, I turn back towards these treelike things lining out the dark and with no more than a step or two, all of the light behind me, at a rate out of proportion to the distance I've come, disappears. To this, I whisper to myself, as much in encouragement as in a soothing of my dejection:

'No matter, son. No matter.'

After these tall shadowy trees fall off and my eyes adapt to an even stonier dark, I realise – if it were possible to say it – that I appear to have become lost.

I stand for some time listening to my heart thump, until I realise that I've gone far too far to have not yet returned to the basilica, so instead, parched and tired, I decide to lie down a while and wait with my eyes opened wide to see if anything of note comes into view.

Lying there, I then wonder, in the darkening moments of Anna's last detachment from us all, will she notice the faintest of earthly tugs, and, if she does, will she be aware of the scale of habit and dumb want circulating in that tug. And if not, then surely she will discern, in the last scintillas of this tug, that it at least belonged to Patricia, a close but soon to be forgotten ally, encountering at last the absence replacing what was once her counterweight.

I wake.

And, for many moments in the half dark, I believe I am back home, in a hotel, on my way to a ruin to see what can be saved of it. Then, in an angled shaft of yellow light, this small golden langur monkey appears once more. I can tell, despite his proximity, that he means me no harm. He is crouched between me and a slim opening, it admitting this slant of wan and uncanny light across the floor. His fingers open and close at his waist in a gesture of hesitation. I sit up on the ground and listen a while, but I can hear nothing. I look to the monkey once more and seeing that he now has his hands up covering his ears, and from his lips and eyes now lifting into a grimace, I can intuit that beyond the opening is a place being filled again with prayer.

This small monkey scampers off; then, two large hands seize me from the floor. My head is forced down as I am lifted to my feet. I am marched, with breath meeting the back of my neck, up some stairs, across an umbrageous hall, through a poorly lit oval room edged with paintings, then up a set of broad and dusty steps, whereupon my head is allowed to rise once more and before me opens out the nave and choir and the transepts of the basilica – this giant inner ear – all bathed again in a glorious morning light. The white archways, sculptures and gold twinkle as a young priest lights a candle to the front of this altar. The smell of incense gathers in spirals up my nose. I am led down the Gospel aisle, dotted with young monks seemingly deep in prayer, but I feel sorry for them all, because they will never see what my mother saw. These men, like me, will never be so brave.

With a degree of roughness I am directed towards two large doors that lead to the narthex and beyond. I can hear the low thrum of morning traffic outside. Both of these hefty doors this priest shoves open with his shoulder. He pauses a moment at the top steps of the church, holding me by the collar of my shirt, as if to present a specimen to those on Via dell'Indipendenza below. The arches and walkways become not passageways, but stilled tribunals, full of people. I blink for some moments and then look across the street, now building with two strips of indifferent and smoking traffic. Then, I see Philomena's face in among the throng of spectators looking on at this priest shoving me onto the steps, all the while chastising me at the top of his voice. I'm no longer listening to this robust middle-aged priest, though; I am looking only at Philomena, who must be by now on her way to work. Her eyebrows knot and her face turns sideways as she comprehends, from across this busy street, precisely what she sees: a dishevelled man, whom she thinks she knows, being thrown from a church and being reprimanded, with increasing anger, for trespassing into this holy place.

13

VIA DELL'OSSERVANZA

The dry heat of late morning beats down once again as I make my way up to our apartment on Via dell'Osservanza. I've left the old-town wall behind and am trudging up the steep incline that leads to our back door. The cicadas overhead are calling out in now near-deafening waves of seemingly contiguous sound.

The priest who was chastising me at the entrance to the basilica became disproportionately angry at my indifference to him, and in a surprisingly old-fashioned act of aggression, he threw me down the steps. I fell and grazed my shin and cut my wrists. Philomena chased across the street and helped me to my feet. She was livid at this middle-aged priest, who did not stay around long after this shoving of me from the door.

Philomena led me to Paninocoteca, where she cleaned up my cuts with serviettes and water. We had a coffee and shared a sandwich. I told her about Anna and the churches I had visited, the monkey and the parrots and the sight of Saint Cecilia. At first she was upset, but as I continued describing to her my day and night and morning, she began to nod more carefully at me, her father's dark-brown eyes taking me in, until, in the end, a painful look of distancing doubt spread into her features. She gave me her phone and asked me to call Bernadette. Bernadette and I spoke for some time, and I apologised to her for not calling, but explained that I'd lost the run of myself thinking about Anna and such related things. Then I told her about the monkey and the parrots and my vision of Saint Cecilia.

After a long pause, she then said down the phone to me, 'That's OK, John; please come home.'

I then asked Philomena if I could charge my phone at her place of work; I said I was expecting an urgent message. But, when we got there, it soon became clear that the shop did not have a suitable adapter for my phone – the brand was too obscure and the model out of date.

Before I turned and left the shop for home, Philomena came over to me and silently wrapped her arms around me. She pulled me to her, with her head then laid upon my chest, and she just held me there to the ground for a time, her eyes winced shut.

She held me there for several beats longer, her eyes closed over to the day.

I round the last corner onto the small road that runs up past the back of our house. I'm glad to see that Francisco is not yet at his workshop today. I don't want to talk to anyone other than Bernadette.

She is standing on the street outside our back door, which is ajar.

And, as I go to her, it becomes clear to me that all connection I have with home is now, or is soon to be, wholly gone, and all I have as connection to the Earth then is here with her. Everything is with her. The closer I get to her and her lovely face, the more I realise it is all the connection I would want, and I am sure that her whispers around me as I go would more than replace as homely any whispers I might have heard while dying in myth at home!

She takes me in her arms, and I can smell her musk and I can tell by the darkness around her eyes that she has not slept since I have last seen her. Her blue eyes seem to have almost smoked, aged over into the beginnings of a greening hazel. I apologise, struggling to look at her directly.

We go upstairs and she pours me a large mug of coffee, which I take at the table in the kitchen among the plants and her stacks of tutorial papers. We sit apart from each other in a formation that might be called suspicious – almost eyeing each other anew. In the light, I can see a single grey follicle arc up from the parting in her hair, like a gunshot over a landscape of fading auburn. Then, despite the strength of the coffee, I suddenly feel incredibly tired.

I say that I would like to lie down for a while.

Bernadette looks to me and nods.

At the door, I stand and turn, as if to say something to her, but I've forgotten what it was. Instead, she comes to me and gives me a gentle kiss on the cheek and asks if I am OK.

'I'm fine,' I say. 'Just tired, now. And you?'

She touches my arm and I rub hers in return. And as I rub her forearm a tear comes to my left eye and as I blink it rolls down my cheek. She rubs my arm until I settle.

I drop the *tenda* down over the bedroom window, take off my boots, remove my shirt and sit down upon our bed. The cicadas outside still call, but they are muted now.

I take my phone out of my pocket, plug it in, turn it on and place it onto my bedside locker.

I recline my head onto a pillow as the phone begins to buzz and fill with messages. The buzzing continues for almost a minute.

Then, I turn onto my stomach and as my breathing deepens I know most of those messages are from Philomena and from Bernadette, and I know too, with a certainty that grows as I fall further towards sleep, that at least one of those buzzing messages is from Patricia, and in it she is informing me – with a degree of happiness, I hope – as to what part of her Anna has disappeared forever and what part is still here with us on the land.

REFERENCES

Tim Ryan and Jurek Kirakowski, *Ballinspittle: Moving
Statues and Faith* (Cork: Mercier Press, 1985)
Michael Klein, *Bettina and Achim*, 1996, bronze public
sculpture in Arnimplatz, Berlin
Uta Ranke-Heinemann, *Eunuchs for the Kingdom of Heaven*
(London: Penguin, 1990)
A. C. Waltham, *Foundations of Engineering Geology*
(Glasgow and London: Blackie A & P, 1994)
Karl Burke, *Omnipresent*, sound sculpture, 2011
Meister Eckhart, *Selected Writings* (London: Penguin
Classics, 1994)
William James, *The Varieties of Religious Experience*
(London: Penguin Classics, 1985 (1902))
Alexander von Humboldt, *Personal Narrative of a Journey
to the Equinoctial Regions of the New Continent* (London:
Penguin Classics, 1995 (1814–25))

ACKNOWLEDGEMENTS

Thank you so much to Niamh Dunphy, Feargal Ward, Penny Price, Nicola Howell Hawley, Andy Williams, Lorenzo Di Calogero-Ross, Ruth Hallinan, Luke Brown, Mehar Anaokar, Georgina Difford and all at Serpent's Tail. My thanks also to Michele, Sean, Emily and all of those at Askeaton Contemporary Arts. Special thanks to Marianne Gunn O'Connor.

I am grateful to the Arts Council of Ireland, from whom I received support while writing this novel.

My thanks also to Profile Books, Tuskar Rock Press and especially Peter Straus.

And finally, my sincere thanks to Colm Tóibín, who edited this book.